The Adventures of Philip and Emery
Volume One

THE ADVENTURES OF PHILIP AND EMERY VOLUME ONE

by

John Paulits

Gypsy Shadow Publishing

The Adventures of Philip and Emery
Volume One
by
John Paulits

Gypsy Shadow Publishing
Lockhart, TX
www.gypsyshadow.com

Library of Congress Control Number: 2019947863

eBook ISBNs (respectively): 9781619500020, 9781619500464, 9781619501317, 9781619500426
Print ISBN: 978-1-61950-355-7

Published in the United States of America

First eBook Edition, Philip and the Haunted House:
September 17, 2011
First Print Edition: August 20, 2019

Contents

Philip and the Haunted House—Page 1
Philip and the Monsters—Page 53
Philip and the Fortune Teller—Page 113
Philip and the Deadly Curse—Page 171
About the Author—Page 213

Philip and the Haunted House
Dedication

To Aunt Marie

CHAPTER ONE

The rumble of a heavy truck caused Philip to turn in his bed and open his eyes. He felt his heart pounding. He had been trapped in some dark, awful house. He immediately recognized his own bedroom and sighed in relief. Only a dream! The sound of the truck stopped briefly and started up again. *Turning a corner*, thought Philip. As he listened, the truck noise ended suddenly, instead of fading little by little. Philip guessed the truck had stopped somewhere in his neighborhood.

He sat up in bed, turned, put his feet on the floor, and stretched. A long Saturday loomed ahead of him. No school. What a great feeling! Philip thought of his dream again. Yesterday, his teacher Mr. Ware read the class the part of *The Adventures of Tom Sawyer* where Tom and Huck look for treasure in the haunted house. While they're looking, they hear someone coming and run upstairs to hide. One of the two men who enter the haunted house turns out to be Injun Joe, who wants to kill Tom for identifying him as Doc Robinson's murderer at Muff Potter's trial. Injun Joe gets suspicious, takes out his knife, and starts to climb the stairs. Tom and Huck lie frozen in fear on the floor, peeking through a chink in the wood as Injun Joe, step by step, gets nearer and nearer. Then, CRASH! The old, rotten stairway collapses and tumbles Injun Joe to the floor.

When Mr. Ware read it, he'd shouted the word "crash" as loud as he could. Everyone, including Philip, jumped out of their chairs. For once he'd been paying close attention, and the teacher rewarded him by almost giving him a heart attack. Philip blamed Mr. Ware for his frightful dream.

How could Tom and Huck even *want* to go inside a haunted house, Philip wondered, even if they thought they'd find some buried treasure? Buried treasure. Philip thought he *might* go into a haunted house to get rich, but not for fun. No way. He decided he'd go back to daydreaming in school next week and stop listening to the teacher's heart-attack reading lessons.

Philip dressed and went downstairs. His father lay on the sofa reading the newspaper.

"Well, look who's awake," his father said, sitting up. "Your mother went to the supermarket. Becky's still sleeping." Becky was Philip's baby sister. "Emery called twice already."

"What time is it, Dad?"

"A little after ten."

He *had* slept a long time. Maybe if he'd gotten up earlier he wouldn't have had the dream about the haunted house. *Stupid reading lesson.*

"Give Emery a call, and I'll get your cereal."

Philip called Emery, who said he'd be right over.

As Philip dropped his cereal bowl into the sink, Emery walked into the kitchen.

"Are you sick?" said Emery.

"No, I'm not sick. Why?"

"You slept so long. I only sleep long if I'm sick. My two baby sisters cry so much I can't sleep late anyway."

"No, I'm not sick. I had this weird dream, though." Philip led Emery into the living room.

"You, too, eh?"

"Me, too? You had a dream?" Philip asked in alarm. *Maybe something's going around*, he thought.

"No, I mean putting the dishes in the sink."

"Oh. Yeah, something new."

"My mother, too. She must have talked to your mother. They do these things together sometimes. What did you dream about?"

"The haunted house Mr. Ware read about yesterday."

"Oh, yeah. When the stairs crashed, and he made everybody jump. Cool!"

"I didn't jump," Philip lied.

"Well, everybody else did. Haunted houses are spooky."

"Only around Halloween," Philip said boldly.

"*All* the time," Emery replied with a sharp nod.

Philip felt he'd established his bravery, so he dropped the topic.

"Weird, though," said Emery.

"What's weird?"

"A big truck pulled up around the corner, and they're taking everything out of the junky, empty house."

"The one with all the grass growing around it?"

"Yeah. It's still got a "Sale" sign on it so I guess nobody bought it yet. That'll be an empty house now and look even *more* haunted."

Philip pictured the house—dark, empty, and surrounded by tall weeds. It *could* be haunted for all he and Emery knew; and there it sat—right around the corner from where they lived.

"Want to go watch them take stuff out?" Emery asked.

"They're still there?"

"Yeah. They only got there a little while ago."

Philip thought of the truck that woke him up.

"Okay," Philip said. He'd go now, but once they'd emptied the house and left it empty and lonely and scary looking, he planned to stay away from it. Far away.

CHAPTER TWO

"What a boring morning," Philip said as he got behind Emery in the lunchroom line to get his milk on Monday.

"Are you getting chocolate or white milk?" asked Emery.

"You know I never get white milk," Philip said, bending into the refrigerated bin to take a milk carton.

"My mother makes me get white milk," Emery reported sadly.

"How'll she know?"

Emery shrugged. "She finds out everything."

Philip ignored Emery's complaint and slid next to him on the bench of their lunch table. "We're partners in the project, right?"

"Yeah, but what are we going to do? It doesn't sound very interesting. I have the list. We'll look at it after we eat." Emery opened his lunch box. "Peanut butter and jelly again. I wish my mother wasn't so busy in the morning with the two babies."

"Why don't you pack your own lunch?" Philip asked as he opened his. "Hey! Where's my sandwich?" He emptied his lunch box onto the cardboard tray the lunch ladies had given him with his milk.

"All you have is an apple and two fig bars?" said Emery, biting into his peanut butter and jelly sandwich and moaning. "Grape jelly, as usual."

"Where's my sandwich?" Philip said, louder than before.

"You sure you had one?"

"Of course I had one." Philip remembered watching his mother make the sandwich. She wrapped it up and handed it to him. He put it into his metal lunch box himself. He left the house and walked to Emery's. He went inside to wait for Emery and left his heavy book bag and the lunch box next to the big bush near the sidewalk. It took about five minutes for Emery and him to come out. He picked up his lunch box and book bag and went to school. He put his lunch box on the shelf in the coat closet, along with everybody else's. Mr. Ware never let anybody go to the closet until lunchtime, and now his sandwich was gone.

"You know," said Emery, "I can see the empty house, a little of it, from my bedroom window."

Hmmmm, Philip mused. The haunted house.

"Emery, I put my lunch box down outside your house today when I went in to get you, and now my sandwich is gone. I never lost a sandwich when people *lived* in the house."

"How could an empty house steal your sandwich?"

"Then you tell me where it went."

"It's probably still at home on your kitchen table. Want half of this?" Emery held out the peanut butter and jelly sandwich. "You can have it for your fig bars."

"Both of them?"

"Well. Okay, one. I don't like it much anyway." They made the exchange and finished their lunches in silence, Philip trying in vain to figure out what happened to his cracked pepper turkey sandwich.

The two boys found a spot in the schoolyard out of the chilly November wind, and Emery took the project list from his back pocket. He unfolded the wrinkled paper.

"So what'll we do?"

Philip still had his mind on his missing sandwich. Thinking about it made him hungry again. Half of Emery's sandwich didn't fill him up. He'd make another sandwich when he got home if he could find any cracked pepper turkey in the refrigerator.

"Mr. Ware said this Community Service project is half our social studies mark, and he spent an awful long time talking about it," said Emery. "My mother's fussy about marks."

"Of course. So's mine. So's everybody's." Philip had sunk into a bad mood because of his missing sandwich. "What's on the list?"

"Okay, listen. Visit sick people in the hospital."

"Yuck. We might catch something, and besides, they didn't even let me in once when my mom and dad went to visit somebody. I had to sit in the lobby and look at a hundred-year-old magazine about furniture."

"All right. Skip the hospital. Hospitals are scary anyway. Visit a homebound elderly."

"A what?"

"A homebound elderly."

They looked at one another in silence.

"Did Mr. Ware explain this one?" Philip wanted to know.

"I think he did. I think it's like some old person who lives alone and never goes out of the house."

"Never?"

"I don't think so."

"So what do they do all day?"

Emery shrugged. "Look out the window, I guess."

Philip paused. "You want to sit and look out a window for social studies?"

"Not much. Sounds pretty easy, but I guess it'd be boring."

"*Way* boring. I don't want to sit and look out a window. What else is there?"

"Raise money for a charity."

"You mean like sell cupcakes or candy."

"I guess."

"Do they give us the candy?"

"I don't think it's a good idea to have you sell candy."

"Why not?"

"Remember you got in trouble before when you sold the candy and kept it after it came. You didn't give it to the people who bought it. You hid it and wanted to eat it all."

"What else is there?" said Philip impatiently, not wanting to be reminded. He hated to eliminate something so promising, though.

"Beautify the neighborhood."

"Go on. What else?

"That's it."

"Only four things?"

"I read the whole list," said Emery, folding up the paper and stuffing it back into his pocket.

"An awful short list," said Philip. "What'll we do?"

"The only thing we didn't cross off was beautifying the neighborhood."

"How do we beautify the neighborhood?"

Emery shrugged. "Maybe you could cover your face."

Philip stared at Emery.

"That was a joke," Emery explained.

"So why didn't you laugh?"

"I'm not supposed to laugh. I made the joke. You're supposed to laugh."

"Ha," Philip burst out, his stare boring into Emery.

"Never mind. You have no sense of humor. Look, let's ask our parents tonight and see what they say."

Philip knew his dad could always come up with something when he got stuck with a school project. He recalled the prize his dad helped him win in the Walk-Mor Shoe Store poster contest. "Good idea. Oh," Philip moaned. "There's the bell already."

Emery and Philip left the sheltered corner of the school building and stepped out into the chilly wind. They ran to where Mr. Ware waited for the class to line up.

CHAPTER THREE

After dinner Philip worked on his homework in his bedroom. He paused when he smelled something funny. He sniffed five, six, seven times. He left his room and went downstairs. His father sat contentedly by the open window in the living room with a big cigar in his mouth! A small fan Philip hadn't seen since the summertime went back and forth on a table blowing air toward his father. Philip watched as his father blew out a straight line of smoke, and the air from the fan caught it and sent it toward the window. Philip watched in fascination as the smoke appeared to melt through the screen.

"Mom's going to be mad," Philip warned. He'd heard his mother and father's cigar conversations before.

"No, she's not," his father answered.

"Why not?"

"She isn't here. She went down to Mrs. Moriarty's for an hour. On purpose."

"She'll smell it when she gets back. She'll be mad."

"She bought it for me."

"No, she didn't."

His father laughed. "I received news at work today. I was selected to be in charge of a very special project. Everyone wanted to be chosen, but they picked me. This..." His father held up the cigar. "...is what your mother gave me as a reward before she left the house."

"Will you get a promotion if you do okay?"

"It is highly likely, Flipster."

"Well, I want one, too," Philip said.

"A cigar?"

"Not a cigar. Blecch! A *promotion*. To fifth grade. Emery and I have to do a project together."

"What's it about?"

Philip went to sit on the sofa far away from his father. "I smelled it upstairs, but I can hardly smell it from here."

"Must be going up to your bedroom window. Better run up and close it, or you'll be smelling it all night."

Philip ran up, closed his window, and hustled back down to the sofa.

"So," said his father. "Your project?"

"Emery and I have to do something helpful for the community. The teacher gave us a list..."

"Say no more. I know exactly what you can do. You're looking for a project idea, right?"

"Yeah, for me and Emery."

"The empty house around the corner is an eyesore. I have to drive past it twice a day, to and from work. If you and Emery cut the grass, it would be a great boon not only to the neighborhood but to mankind in general."

"Cut the grass? I don't think..."

"Call Emery. Tell him you've got the most absolutely A+ idea."

"But nobody lives there. We can't get permission. We can't..."

"No problem. I'll call the real estate agent tomorrow and explain the circumstances. He'd be positively delirious if someone made that place look better. He's trying to sell the place, Philip. The better it looks; the better for him."

"But I don't think cutting grass..."

"You can use my mower, my clippers. Emery's family has a mower, too. You and Emery've helped me with the lawn before. You're both experienced clip-masters. Flipster, you're in for an exciting Saturday. We'll take before and after pictures, and you can write up a report. Your teacher will be astonished at your fine work."

Philip frowned. He couldn't even get an argument going with his father. He didn't want anything to do with the empty house. More than his sandwich might disappear if he started hanging around *there.*

"So, it's settled. Now scoot. You're interrupting my reward. Go. Go, call Emery. Give him the good news."

Philip shuffled into the kitchen and picked up the phone.

When Emery answered, Philip could hear babies crying in the background.

"Oh, hi, Philip."

"Your parents have any good ideas for the project?"

"I didn't ask yet. I'm waiting till my sisters go to sleep. Did you ask?"

"My dad wants us to cut the grass in front of the haunted house and make it look less haunted."

"He called it a haunted house?"

"Not those exact words, but same idea."

The conversation halted while Emery thought the suggestion over. "Well, I guess it's better than all those other things."

"But the place is so scary," said Philip.

"Not when it's light out, and it'll be a Saturday afternoon when people are walking around. You know... it sounds easy. You don't want to visit a hospital or sit next to an old person and look out the window, do you?"

"No. You sure the candy sale's no good?"

"You think your parents would let you?"

"No, I guess not."

"So?"

"Well, I guess it'll be all right. I'll see if I can get my dad to stay with us while we work. Hey! Maybe the real estate guy will say no, and we won't even have to do it. It's not our property, you know."

"If he does say no, we'll have to pick one of those other things."

The boys said goodbye. Philip hoped the real estate man would tell them to stay away. Thinking of something else would be safer and easier than spending a whole day working around a haunted house.

CHAPTER FOUR

Philip knew when he went to bed Friday night this would be the first Saturday he didn't look forward to since school started. The real estate agent had given his father permission to cut the grass in front of the haunted house. His father had given Emery and him refresher lessons on how to safely operate the lawn mowers and had bought a disposable camera for the before and after pictures. Philip thought things over and promised himself he'd never *ever* volunteer for any kind of community service again unless he had to—like now. What a Saturday *this* would be. He couldn't wait for Sunday.

"Time to get up, my little neighborhood improvement elf." Philip opened his eyes and saw his father standing at the foot of his bed.

"I think I'm sick. I have pneumonia or something." Philip coughed as hard as he could.

"No weaseling out. You're about to do a good deed and get a super A+. Up. Let's go. I called Emery. We meet him outside his house in twenty minutes."

Thirty minutes later they stood in front of the haunted house.

"Now, you guys get on the front lawn in the middle... there... where the grass is the highest. There are twelve pictures on this camera I bought for you, so I'll take six now and six when you finish and get them developed right away. Look on the bright side! You'll be all done with your project by Monday, and the rest of your class will still be struggling."

Emery and Philip silently trudged to the spot on the lawn in the high grass Philip's father had indicated.

Emery looked down. "What's that?"

Philip bent down and gingerly picked up a dirty, damp white sock.

"Put that down," Philip's father snapped. "I don't want a picture of an old sock. Here, use these gardening gloves to clean things up so you can mow." Mr. Felton reached into a large paper bag and took out two pairs of brown cloth gloves. "A pair for you; a pair for you. Anything you need to pick up use them and one of these." A handful of large black trash bags came out of the paper bag next.

Philip and Emery looked at each other.

"This is getting complicated. I don't think I'm going to like this," said Emery.

"I already don't like it," Philip grumped.

"Okay. Smile!"

After Philip's father moved the boys to five other spots for five more pictures, he said, "Okay, let's see you turn on the mowers. Turn the key and push the button."

The boys obeyed, and both machines roared to life.

Philip's father drew his finger across his throat, and the boys turned the machines off. "First, go over the lawn and pick up anything in the mower's way. You don't want pieces of old sock or any tin cans flying around."

"Suppose there's yucky stuff on the lawn," Philip said warily.

His father pointed to the brown gloves Philip held. "When the lawn is clean, start the mowers and get to work. Your lunches are in this bag." A smaller paper bag came out of the larger one. "I'll put it here out of the sun." Mr. Felton walked to the shady porch of the house and put the bag down. Emery and Philip both wondered which of them would be the one to go retrieve it.

"It's ten-thirty. I'll be back in an hour to see how much progress you've made. Eat when you get hungry. Good luck." Philip's father walked down the street toward the corner and home, leaving the two boys standing in the high grass feeling very alone.

Emery said, "Did I hear your dad whistling? He's awful happy."

"If you were going back home, you'd be whistling, too."

"I guess. Pshew! Look at this place."

The two boys turned their eyes away from Philip's departing father and looked over their chore. They stood in the deep grass before a two-story house in need of a lot of painting. Two broken chairs sat on the porch, along with the brown paper bag with the boys' lunches. The front door of the house had a long, oval window in it looking like a black, shadowy mouth stretched open in a weird, scary shape.

They inspected the lawn again. The grass was green in spots but a lot of it had turned brown and crackly. A cement walkway leading to the porch separated the plot of grass on the right from one on the left. Fortunately, whoever had lived there before paved over behind the house to park their car, so no grass at all grew there.

"Well," said Philip, "you take one side and I'll do the other."

"There's an awful lot of grass," said Emery. Then both boys noticed how quiet the neighborhood had grown; no bird sounds, no people and very few cars.

"You sure you don't want to go visit old people?" Emery asked in a small voice. "Maybe they'll just like fall asleep while they look out the window, and all we'll have to do is keep them from falling out of their chairs."

"Oh, come on. It's too late now. Let's get started. I'll start over there." Philip walked across the concrete walkway and into the high grass. When he turned, Emery stood right behind him.

Philip jumped. "Emery! Get over there. Get your mower and start over there."

"Why don't we work together? We could both push one mower and then we could go faster."

"We have two mowers. We'll finish faster if you do that side and I do this side."

Suddenly a noise came from somewhere the boys couldn't locate.

"Did you hear?" Emery said, stepping closer to Philip.

"All right. All right. We'll push together. The tall grass is probably hard to cut."

"Yeah, right. I think you're right. Good idea. Go ahead. Turn on the mower."

Philip stepped up to the mower, Emery right at his elbow.

Philip looked at him. "Could you move a little please?"

"Move where?"

"Away from me a little."

"Why?"

"You're breathing on me."

"If I stop breathing can I stay close?"

"You can breathe, just don't get so close. I need some room to turn the mower on." Emery took a half step back.

Philip turned the key and pushed the button, and suddenly they were surrounded by noise. Philip shouted at Emery, "Come on. Hold on here and push with me."

Emery got elbow-to-elbow with Philip, and the two friends pushed the mower through the tall grass. Their community improvement project was underway.

CHAPTER FIVE

The two busy boys had finished one side of the lawn, raked up the loose grass and put it into big, black trash bags and had begun the second side of the lawn when Philip's father returned carrying a jug. Philip turned the mower off when he saw him.

"What's in there?" Philip asked.

"Your mom made you some lemonade. I see you're sweating. Why don't you stop for lunch and have some of this lemonade to cool off?"

"I'm hungry," Emery said. He wiped his sleeve across his forehead. "I didn't think I could sweat so much when it wasn't summer."

Philip's father laughed. "You're doing a good day's work, Emery. Run and get your lunch."

Emery looked at Philip and both boys knew without saying anything they would go to the porch *together* to pick up their lunch. They walked toward the porch step-by-step, shoulder-to-shoulder. When they reached the porch steps, they stared in surprise.

"Where is it?" Emery whispered. He and Philip looked right, then left. Philip waved his hand to Emery, and they walked up the three steps onto the porch and looked right and left again. The brown paper bag wasn't there.

"Dad," Philip called.

"Shhh! Not so loud," Emery warned, keeping his eyes on the front door and the two dark windows on each side of it.

"Dad," Philip called more quietly. "The lunches are missing."

Philip's father walked up the path and looked for the lunch bag. "I put it right there. Funny. Did you guys see a dog or something walking around up here?"

"*Something?*" Emery repeated. He grabbed Philip's elbow, and they backed slowly off the porch.

"That's the second time my lunch has disappeared," Philip whispered. "You *know* I didn't leave it in the kitchen this time, Emery."

"I know. I know," said Emery, his eyes darting everywhere.

"Did you?" Mr. Felton repeated.

"Did I what?" Philip asked.

"See a dog."

"Dog? No, no dog."

"Funny," Mr. Felton repeated. "Well, look. Have some lemonade, and I'll go home and make two more sandwiches. I'll be right back."

"How about if we come with you?" Emery blurted, stepping closer to Philip's father. Philip moved with him.

"Yeah," said Philip. "Then you won't have to carry it back."

"Save you some time," Emery added.

"All right. Come on. And let me tell you, you're doing a good job on this lawn. Come home, have lunch, and then get this finished up. I'll come back with the camera and take the 'after' photos, and your project will be done."

The boys stayed close to Mr. Felton and home they went.

Finally, at three o'clock as Philip tied up the last big garbage bag full of grass—"haunted grass"—the boys called it, Philip's father showed up, camera in hand.

"Wow," he said. "What a difference. Now go stand in the same six places you stood before, and I'll take six pictures. If this doesn't get you an A+ I'll be very surprised."

Philip and Emery hurried to one spot after another, posing once with a lawnmower in front of them; once holding rakes; three times with their arms across each other's shoulders; and in the final photo surrounded by four big, black trash bags. They were finished.

"Okay, let's go," said Emery.

"Yeah, Dad. We're done. Nothing left to do."

"Let's put these trash bags by the curb for the trash truck and we'll go."

Philip and Emery each dragged a trash bag to the curb while Philip's father dragged the other two.

"That's everything, let's go," said Philip's father. "Grab the mowers. I'll get the two rakes. We'll put this stuff back into our garages, then drive to the mall to drop the film off."

"Can we go to the arcade in the mall for a while?" Philip asked.

"I think you've earned it," said Mr. Felton as they transported their equipment down the street. "And my treat, five dollars each—a reward for a job well done."

Philip and Emery looked at each other. "All right," they shouted and slapped hands. The haunted house slowly slipped out of their memories.

CHAPTER SIX

"I'm going to bed," Philip reported to his parents, who sat on the living room sofa watching TV.

"So soon?" Philip's mother asked in surprise. "It's not even nine o'clock yet."

"I'm tired. And everything hurts," Philip grumbled.

"Are you getting sick?" asked his mother, beginning to get up, but Mr. Felton put out his hand and made her sit back down.

"Philip is suffering from what is known as a hard day's work. Don't you worry, Flipster. The achiness goes away, but the good job you did today will last. At least until the grass grows back."

"I don't want to do it again," said Philip in alarm.

His father laughed. "No, you're right. Once was enough. The weather's changing anyway. The grass probably won't grow any more till spring. Go on to bed. We'll see you in the morning."

"Don't forget to brush your teeth," said his mother.

Philip brushed his teeth, got into his pajamas, and climbed into bed. He couldn't remember ever being so tired. He closed his eyes. As he started to drift off to sleep, the sound of sirens floated up to him from the street, but he felt too tired to wonder why they sounded so close. He just didn't care.

The next morning Philip lay on the living room floor reading the Sunday comics when the phone rang. He answered and heard Emery's voice.

"Did you hear about the robbery last night?"

"No, I kind of went to bed early. What robbery?"

"The pizza store across the street from school. The two robbers took a lot of money."

"How do you know?"

"My dad heard it on the radio. I even heard the sirens last night."

"Oh, yeah. Me, too. Is that what they were for? I heard them when I went to bed."

"That was only like nine o'clock. You went to bed so early?"

"All the lawn mowing."

"Yeah, I went to bed at nine-thirty," Emery confessed. "What'll we do today? Hey, did your dad get the pictures back yet?"

"No, not till Monday, he said."

"Oh. So what'll we do today?"

"I was thinking about the haunted house. Let's pack another lunch and put it on the porch. Then we make believe we're going away, but really hide across the street. Maybe we can see what happens to it."

"You want to see the ghost?"

"Ghost! Don't be dumb. It can't be a ghost. My lunches disappeared during the day. Ghosts only come out at night, right?"

"Maybe it's a daytime ghost."

"A daytime ghost? What's a daytime ghost?"

"You know. If you die at night, you're a nighttime ghost. If you die during the day, you're a daytime ghost."

"Is that true? You sure?"

Emery shrugged. "All the ghosts can't be flying around at night. They'd bump into one another. Some must have to fly around in the daytime so it's not so crowded."

"How many ghosts do you think there are, anyway?"

"Lots."

"It couldn't be a ghost though, could it?" Philip reasoned. "Ghosts don't eat, right?"

"This one ate our sandwiches."

Philip pondered the possibility. "Anyway, let's put the sandwich on the porch, then hide and see what happens."

"How far away will we hide?"

"Far enough to be safe."

"Where's that? Alaska?"

"No, not Alaska. Across the street."

"You sure across the street is safe?"

"It should be. We were closer than that when the second lunches got stolen, and the ghost didn't do anything to us."

"Hey, you said it *wasn't* a ghost."

"All right, no ghost. We'll be safe from whatever took them."

"*Whatever* took them! What kind of whatever you mean?"

"How do I know what kind of whatever? A whatever's just a whatever. Something took them, right?"

"Oh, great. I'd rather it was a ghost than a whatever that took them."

"We'll be far away and safe."

"We better be."

"Don't worry."

"Pack the lunch and come by for me. I'll be waiting. And worrying."

Ten minutes later the two boys walked down Pratt Street toward the haunted house.

"It's kind of hard to tell the house is haunted after we cut the grass," Emery said.

"Shhh," whispered Philip. They'd reached the beginning of the cement walkway. "Here." He handed the brown bag to Emery.

"Here, what? What do you mean 'here?' I don't want it. You take it."

"I'll be your lookout. If I yell, you start running."

"How about I be *your* lookout and if *I* yell, *you* start running?"

"I yell better than you," Philip claimed.

"Oh, no. I yell pretty good, too. Want to hear?"

"No, no, shhhh!" Philip sighed in exasperation. "All right. We'll both go."

"If we both go, who's going to yell so we can both start running?"

"We'll both yell, and we'll both start running."

"Which way shall we run?"

"Away, away! We'll run away! Now, come on." Shoulder-to-shoulder the two boys took tiny steps up the walkway. They looked left, right, and everywhere, ready to yell and ready to run. They saw nothing to yell about, though, and when they got near the porch Philip underhanded the lunch to the same spot as yesterday's lunch.

"Good throw," said Emery. "Let's go." They backed down the walkway until they reached the sidewalk.

"Now what?" Emery whispered.

"Just act normal."

"Walking backwards isn't normal."

"So let's turn around."

"If we turn around we can't watch the house."

Philip's voice rose in exasperation. "Well, we can't walk all the way to the corner backwards, can we? We'll look stupid. Let's turn together. We can hide behind the house across the street and watch what goes on. Ready?"

The boys turned slowly and walked down the street, Emery sneaking peeks over his shoulder until Philip told him to stop. They crossed the street and went a little way down the block. When they'd gone far enough, they turned and went behind the house directly across from the haunted house.

"Suppose the people who live here see us," Emery said in a worried voice.

"Be quiet and nobody will know."

"Peek out. Can you see it from here?" Emery asked.

Philip moved back and forth and finally stepped out from behind the house. "Emery," Philip said, his voice rising softly, "it's not there."

"The house isn't there! Are you crazy? What are you talking about?"

"No dummy, not the house, the lunch. How could the house not be there? The lunch isn't where I threw it."

"It has to be. I saw you throw it. Look again."

Philip stepped away from the house. "Nope, I don't see it. Come on." The boys walked alongside the house and onto the sidewalk. They crossed the street and paused at the beginning of the cement walkway. Shoulder-to-shoulder, they repeated their march along the walkway.

"Where is it?" Emery whispered. "See it anywhere?"

Philip's heart thumped like it was jumping up and down trying to put out a fire in his chest. Suddenly, a gust of breeze blew a piece of paper from the porch toward the boys. The paper landed at Emery's feet, and he bent to pick it up.

Emery studied the paper and held it in front of Philip. "Philip, did you put a Happy Pie in this lunch?"

"I put blueberry," he gulped, staring at the wrapper in Emery's hand. "That's a blueberry Happy Pie paper." Philip took a step backward, and Emery stepped back with him.

In a rising voice ending in a scream Emery cried, "Philip, something ate the Happy Pie. Let's get out of here!"

Philip didn't have to be told twice. Off the boys ran at top speed, and they didn't stop until they reached Philip's living room.

CHAPTER SEVEN

"Before we go home today," Mr. Ware began, "we have time to check on how some of you are coming with your community service project."

Emery's hand shot up, and Mr. Ware said, "Yes, Emery?"

"We're finished. Philip and me."

Mr. Ware raised his eyebrows. "So soon? What was your project?"

Emery said proudly, "We beautified the neighborhood."

The class giggled, and Philip slunk down in his seat.

"And how did you beautify the neighborhood? Give us a preview of your report. We have a little time now," Mr. Ware said with a smile.

Emery told their story, leaving out any suggestion about the house being haunted and about the disappearing lunches. He ended, "And we'll be getting the before and after pictures tonight. Philip's dad is bringing them home after his work."

"Well, very impressive, Emery, Philip. The rest of you, class, still have time, though. And you two boys can still try to add to yours, improve it if you can think of a way, but it sounds very good as it is. Anyone have any questions?"

Since the hands of the clock showed three o'clock, no one was dumb enough to prolong the school day by asking a question, so Mr. Ware dismissed the class.

Emery asked his mother's permission to have dinner at Philip's house so he would be there when Philip's father got home from work with the photographs. On their way home they peeked down Pratt Street toward the haunted house, but nothing unusual met their cautious eyes.

"What's your mom cooking tonight?" Emery asked as the two boys opened their book bags and got right to their homework.

"I don't know."

"Aren't you two going out to play?" Philip's mom asked when she saw them.

Even though Pratt Street had looked like any normal street, and even though the weather outside made for a very lovely November day, the boys decided to stay inside.

"No, we have homework, Mom. What's for dinner?"

"Well, since your father had to stop by the mall to pick up your photos, we decided he'd bring home some Chinese food for dinner. Mom's night off."

"Fortune cookies, too?" Philip asked. "And those crispy noodles with the sweet sauce?"

"I think your father's lived with you long enough, Philip, to know. Don't worry."

Philip and Emery slapped hands and got to work. They took a break at four-thirty to watch The Three Stooges on TCM for half-an-hour, but by the time Philip's dad walked in at five forty-five, they'd finished with their homework.

"Did you get the pictures, Dad? Let me see," said Philip.

"Here they are," Mr. Felton said, putting down the big bag of Chinese food and reaching into his briefcase. He tossed the bag of photographs to Philip, who curled up on the sofa with Emery to look them over. Mr. Felton hung up his coat, and carried the wonderful smelling bag of food to the kitchen.

"Wow," said Emery. "They look good. You look stupid in this one with your foot on the bag of grass. You look like you're Tarzan, and you killed it or something."

Philip felt silly when he looked at the picture, but Emery was right. The pictures did look good. "We're getting an A for sure."

"Did you write up our report?" Emery asked.

"Most of it. I can write the rest now we have the pictures. You know, put those words at the bottom of the pictures."

"Captions," Emery explained.

"What?"

"Captions. They're called captions."

"Oh." Philip thought a moment. "If you know what they're called, why don't you write them?"

Emery thought a moment. "I know what a rocket ship is, but I can't build one. I know what a home run is, but I can't hit one. I know what a poem is, but I can't write one. I know what Chinese food is..."

"All right. All right. I get it."

Philip's mom called that dinner would be ready in five minutes.

Philip looked over the pictures again and began to arrange them for the report.

"These two go together," said Emery when he saw Philip matching the photos.

"I know. I know. And this one..." Philip stopped. He picked up one of the photos from the sofa cushion and held it close to his eyes. He took the companion picture and studied it even more closely. He picked up two more and put them aside. He picked up another two and after them another two. After he'd inspected all the photos, he kept one pair in his hand and put another pair down in front of him.

"What's wrong?" Emery asked.

"Emery..." Philip began.

"Philip, what?"

"Look at these two pictures."

Emery took them and studied them. "Yeah, so?"

"You know those puzzles? Like in the Sunday comics. Find six things different from one picture to another?"

"Yeah."

"Find one thing different from this picture to this one."

"The grass is cut."

"Don't be stupid. Would I ask you if it was that easy?"

Emery tried again.

"We're standing in a little different spot?"

Philip glared at his friend.

Emery defended himself and said, "Well, in those comic puzzles some of the things are only changed real little. A finger moved and stuff like that."

"Look at the porch."

"The porch. Okay, I'll look at the porch."

Philip waited.

"Yeah. There's something. A piece of paper."

"Right. Look close. I think it's a Happy Pie paper."

Emery looked close.

"Maybe, but it's just a regular piece of paper."

"You see the color?"

"Mmmm," said Emery, concentrating on the picture. "It's Happy Pie colors."

"My mom put Happy Pies in our missing lunches. Remember?"

"So the... whatever ate the pie and threw away the paper?"

"You think I'm kidding? The whatever ate the pie the second time when we tried to catch it, didn't it?"

"Don't call it an 'it.' I don't like... it."

Philip frowned at Emery. "Now look at this." He handed Emery two more pictures.

Emery looked at them carefully. He looked up at Philip, his eyes wide.

"Even you see this one, don't you?"

"The window's open," said Emery softly. "It's not open in the first picture, and it's open in the second." There were windows on each side of the front door, and one of the windows had opened itself very slightly in between when Philip's father took the first picture and when he took the second picture.

"Why is the window open, Emery?"

"Maybe the whatever wanted some fresh air?"

"I think *you* need some fresh air. No. The window's open because this house has to be haunted, Emery," Philip said decisively. "Windows don't open by themselves."

Emery looked again at the second picture. Without doubt, someone or... some*thing* opened the window while he and Philip cut the grass.

"Dinner, boys. Come and get it," called Philip's mom.

Philip turned the photos upside-down on the coffee table. "We'll figure this out later. Let's go eat," he said and led Emery into the kitchen.

CHAPTER EiGHT

As Philip went upstairs to take his bath later, he heard his parents talking in the living room. It sounded interesting so he sat on the next to the top step to listen.

"They haven't caught them yet," his father said.

"You don't think they'd start robbing houses, do you?" his mother asked.

"Probably not. Not enough money in them. They made off with quite a bit from the pizza store Saturday night and the deli the day before. The paper said the police think the robbers might actually be from this neighborhood since they seem to know it so well."

"Can't they trace the money and arrest them when they spend it?"

Philip's father shrugged. "Maybe. They can if they know the serial numbers, but it's not likely the store owners wrote them down."

"No, I suppose not," Philip's mother answered.

Philip heard someone get up so he got up, too, and went into the bathroom. He turned on the water for his bath and began to think. As he sat in the bathtub, he thought some more. Usually he found some way to play in the water, but this time he didn't bother playing. He simply sat and thought. After he dried off and got into his pajamas, he went downstairs to say goodnight to his parents. He climbed back up to his room, turned off the lights, nestled into bed, and thought some more. Soon, he had it all figured out. He had a plan, but he'd need Emery's help because he knew he couldn't act out his plan all by himself. No way.

As Philip slept, he dreamed he moved toward a very dark place with something close behind him. He turned and saw another boy his size. It had to be Emery. Together they moved into the dark place. An odd noise sounded nearby. He turned to the boy next to him but couldn't see the boy's face. Together, they moved forward. Suddenly, a bright shape came at them from the right. The boys ducked. Then a bright shape came from the left. They ducked again. Philip turned and a bright shape came from behind them. He and the other boy ran. The other boy pointed. Ahead of them lay a golden object. They ran to it, and the other boy picked it up. More bright shapes came at them. He and the other boy ducked and ran faster and faster toward a light gleaming ahead of them. The bright shapes chasing them disappeared as they approached the light, and the other boy still had it—the golden treasure.

Philip's eyes opened, and he could feel his heart beating hard. Why? Oh, his dream. Then he remembered it. All of it. A dream about entering a scary place and coming out of it with a treasure. Two boys, like Tom and Huck. But this time—him and Emery! In the haunted house! The dream made him certain what he'd planned earlier would work! The haunted house *had* to be the place where the bandits who robbed the neighborhood stores hid the stolen money, especially if, as his father said, they knew the neighborhood. The opened window in the photograph proved someone—and not a whatever—used the house. It had to be the robbers. Who else could it be? Wait until he told Emery what he'd figured out! They had a chance to be rich! They could get the money when the crooks weren't looking. It would be easy. He only had to convince Emery to go inside the haunted house with him, and he'd do that in school today.

$$\text{\ding{167} \quad \ding{167} \quad \ding{167}}$$

"Let's walk past the haunted house," said Philip as he and Emery walked home from school.

Emery stopped. "Why?"

"I want to tell you something about the haunted house."

"Same side of the street or across?"

"Across," Philip answered more quickly than he meant to. He'd never convince Emery to go inside with him if he acted afraid of the house.

As they walked, Philip talked. He told his friend everything he figured out the night before. By the time they stood opposite the house, Philip had said all he needed to. With its newly mown lawn and with the bright November sun shining, the house looked peaceful.

"The window's closed," Emery said.

"I see." It was the first thing Philip had looked for.

Emery went on. "You really think the crooks hid the money inside the house?"

"*Somebody* opened the window, right?"

"But if we go in to get the money, won't they be in there and get us?"

"No, I told you. You don't think they stay there all the time, do you? Somebody would see them. Somebody would see them go in and out if they were there all the time. They can't cook there or anything like that. And if a grownup saw the window down and up and then down again, the grownup would investigate or call the police."

"I'll bet they can't even flush the toilet."

Philip looked at Emery.

"Somebody might hear it."

"So there you go. They were there on Saturday when we cut the grass because they committed a robbery on Friday night. They hid the money and went away. They did it again on Sunday afternoon when they threw away the Happy Pie paper. There's got to be a lot of money in there, Emery."

"When we get it, do we put it in the bank or what do we do with it? Can we go out and spend it?"

"I don't think we could spend so much money. Thousands and thousands of dollars."

Pronouncing such a vast amount silenced the boys as they contemplated the wonder of it.

"Do we have to give it back?" Emery asked. "If we know it's stolen money and we keep it, can't we go to jail?"

"You always make problems," Philip grumped. But he didn't have an answer. "I'll ask my dad. Even if we have to give it back, we'll probably get a reward. A big reward."

"Can't we *tell* the police where the money is and let them get it?"

"They won't believe us, and suppose *they* get the reward then. And besides we won't know where it is unless we go in and find it. It could be upstairs, downstairs, in the basement. Let's find it first, and we can decide what to do second."

Emery started across the street.

"Where are you going?" Philip asked.

"Aren't we going to look for the money?"

"Are you crazy? Not now. We can't let anyone see us go in there. We'll get chased or somebody'll follow us in, and *they'll* find the money instead of us. We have to pick a right time."

"I like now," said Emery. "It's light out and there's lots of people around."

"But we don't know if they robbed any place last night. If they did, they might be in there hiding *more* money."

"Oh. Maybe." Emery examined the house. "I don't see anyone."

"Of course you don't see anyone," Philip cried in exasperation. "You think they sit at the windows and wave hello to people?"

"How can we know when to go in?"

"It has to be after a day when they didn't commit a robbery."

"It could be today," Emery said.

"But we're not sure. Look, let's both listen to the radio before we go to school tomorrow. If there's another robbery around here, it will on the radio. Remember, as soon as you wake up, turn on the radio, and if there was no robbery, we'll sneak around back tomorrow after school and see if we can find a way in."

Both boys felt a chill as they thought of what they planned to do.

"Let's get out of here," said Philip. "We'll look suspicious if we stand around much longer." He and Emery turned and, filled with thoughts of what tomorrow might bring, walked the rest of the way home.

CHAPTER NINE

"Dad, were there any more robberies?" Philip tried to sound casual as he asked the question.

"Robberies?"

"You know. Like the two in the neighborhood, the pizza store and the sandwich store."

"Oh. No, not since Saturday night."

Philip thought a minute. "Did they catch the bad guys yet?"

"I don't think so." Philip's father sat reading the newspaper. The family had finished dinner, and his mother had gone down to Mrs. Moriarty's house.

"What's the newspaper say?"

"Nothing about any more robberies." His father folded the newspaper onto his lap. "What's up?"

"Do you know if there's a reward? You know, if someone found the money and gave it back."

"I don't know, but it's likely the stores would show their gratitude. Why? You got a lead in the case?"

Philip stomach jumped. He looked at his father, but saw he was only kidding.

"Suppose someone found the money and kept it?"

"I think they could land in lots of trouble if they did."

"Would they go to jail?"

"It's possible."

Philip didn't like the sound of that. He and Emery would have to be satisfied with the reward. Philip's father opened up his newspaper again, and Philip made his way up to his room. There was nothing to do now but to listen to the radio tomorrow morning.

"This is WIBG in beautiful Brunton, Pennsylvania. The temperature is a seasonable 46 degrees. At the tone the time will be 8 o'clock. *Beep.* And now the news."

Philip listened to stories about Washington, President Obama, the Middle East and something about wrangling over debt.

"And now your local news."

Philip sat up and gave the radio every ounce of his attention. The Mayor did this. Somebody else did that. Something about school taxes. A story about a lady whose cat got stuck in a tree for two whole days. Philip knew when they got to the cat story the serious news was over. He sighed with relief. He dashed back to his room and stuck his flashlight into his book bag. They'd need it if they had to go down into the haunted house basement.

Philip racked his brain, but couldn't come up with anything else they might need. He'd told his mother he'd be at Emery's house after school, but he knew as soon as he and Emery dropped off their book bags, their adventure would begin.

"How long do you think this'll take?" Emery asked as he and Philip huddled together in a bush behind the haunted house.

"I don't know. Why?"

"I don't want to be in there when it gets dark."

"No, no. Me either," Philip admitted. He looked at his watch. "It won't take that long. We have plenty of time."

"You sure?"

"Yeah."

"How do we get in?"

"How do I know?"

"Kind of important."

"Yeah, real. Look, if the front windows went up and down, maybe the back windows go up and down, too."

"Maybe the back door's even unlocked," Emery said hopefully.

Both boys eyed the house carefully.

"We know we can't go in the front way. Somebody might see us," Philip said.

"Somebody could see us go in the back way, too."

"We have to go in some way," Philip said impatiently. "We can't go down the chimney."

Emery looked up. "There's a chimney?"

"No, there's no chimney!" Philip barked.

"Shhhh," Emery warned, his finger to his lips.

"Shhh yourself. Don't talk. Think." The two boys studied the back of the house again.

A cement backyard filled the space between the bushes where they hid and the back door. The back door had a block of four small windows in it, and the back wall of the house had two sets of bigger windows.

"What'll we do if everything's locked up?" Emery whispered.

Philip ignored the grim question and whispered back, "Come on. You try one window and I'll try the other." Philip bent over as far as he could and still keep his balance and ran to the window on the left. He pushed against it, but it wouldn't move. He noticed Emery standing by the back door. Emery waved him over.

"Broken window," said Emery.

Philip looked and saw a hole in the window nearest the doorknob. He watched Emery reach his hand inside the broken window. "I saw," Emery said as he wiggled his arm around, "my father...do this...where is it...here...when he locked everybody out once." Emery carefully removed his arm from the broken window as the back door swung slightly open.

"You opened it," said Philip in amazement. "Quick; in!" He pushed Emery ahead of him and pushed the door closed. Both boys stood statue-still. They were *inside* the haunted house.

CHAPTER TEN

"At least it's bright in here," said Emery. The afternoon light filled up the kitchen, and through the kitchen entryway they could see the dining room.

"They probably wouldn't hide the money in a place everybody could see," Philip said.

"'Loot'," corrected Emery. "I read stolen money is called 'loot.'"

'Loot'. Philip liked the sound. He regretted not using the word. "Well," he whispered, "the loot is probably in a dark place. Come on; and stay away from the windows." He bent way over and tiptoed out of the kitchen into the dining room. He pointed to a door. "Basement. The loot's probably down there."

Emery took a deep breath. "Can we turn the basement light on? Will anybody outside see it?"

Philip scrunched his forehead together. "I don't remember if there's any window to the basement. Do you?"

Emery scrunched his eyes closed. "I don't remember."

"All right. Let's go down the basement and see if there are any windows. If there aren't, we can come back up and turn on the lights."

"Good idea. Go ahead."

"You go first."

"No, you. You have the flashlight."

Philip remembered the heavy object in his right hand. He'd reminded himself over and over to let to Emery carry it, but in all of the excitement, he forgot to hand it over. Now he was stuck.

Philip waved his left hand to Emery in exasperation as he moved in the lead and put his hand on the doorknob. "Ready?"

"I guess." Emery pointed to kitchen and the back door. "Are you gonna yell and then we run or should I yell and then we run?"

"Who cares who yells?"

"Well, last time you wanted to..."

"Never mind last time. Just run if something goes wrong."

"Shouldn't we yell, too?"

"So yell, if you want."

"Should we yell first and then run, or run first and then yell?"

"Yell whenever you want to yell! Just be quiet now, okay?"

"Sheesh. Don't get mad."

"You ready? Here I go," Philip whispered. He took his hand off the doorknob and wiped his palm. "Shall I throw it open fast or open it really slow?"

Emery thought a moment. "Fast," he whispered. "If anything is there, it'll be surprised and make a noise and we'll hear it and run. And yell. If you open it slow, it won't hear us and we'll walk right into it."

"Don't say 'it.'"

"Whatever will hear us then."

"Don't say whatever."

"Some nice polite robber will be waiting for us. How's that? Better?"

Philip rolled his eyes and reached out for the doorknob again. He looked at Emery. "Ready?" he whispered in his quietest voice yet.

"I'm ready. I'm ready."

Without speaking, Philip mouthed the numbers, "One, two..." He swallowed, took a deep breath, and yanked open the door.

Both boys screamed. Something awful did wait on the other side of the door! Something legless and headless! They froze to the spot, their hearts pounding, waiting for their stomachs to bounce back up from the floor.

"Oh!" Emery cried in relief. "It's an old raincoat. You picked a closet door. What'd you pick a closet door for?"

Philip closed the door and caught his breath. He felt like he'd run around the block with a maniac chasing him.

"You didn't tell me not to, did you?" He waved his hand at Emery again. "Come on."

They found another door off the living room. This time Philip opened the door slowly. A black tunnel descended before him.

"This is no closet," Philip whispered over his shoulder. He could see halfway down the stairs, the lower half lost in the black of the basement. He looked at Emery and pointed down, telling Emery to go ahead. Emery shook his head and pointed at the flashlight in Philip's hand.

Philip kicked himself again and snapped on the flashlight, which made a dim, wide, yellow circle on the distant basement floor. In single file, the two boys moved down the stairs until they stood at the bottom.

"Shine the light around and see if there's a window," said Emery.

Philip played the light over the walls, but this basement, like his and Emery's basements, had no windows.

"Go up and turn on the lights," said Philip.

A moment later, *light*. Beautiful light. Emery ran down the stairs. The boys looked at each other and smiled. Now they could take their time and search the basement in this beautiful, safe light.

"Let's start looking," said Philip.

"Let's look together," said Emery, afraid Philip might say, "You start here and I'll start there."

"Yeah, together—same way we mowed the grass. It's our lucky way of working."

"Good idea," said Emery.

Philip waved Emery forward. "Let's start there and..." A dull noise stopped them in their tracks. They peeked at each other, afraid to turn around. Something made a clear, louder noise behind them.

It came again. Louder.

They slowly turned and saw a man tucked in under the stairway they'd come down. He sat on a thin mattress, rubbing his eyes as if he'd just woke up. He had a messy gray beard and messy, long gray hair. He had on a pair of jeans torn at both knees, and his T-shirt had a faded picture of Winnie-the-Pooh on it. He lowered his hands and looked at the boys in amazement.

"Uh, oh," the man said. He got to his feet.

Philip and Emery looked at each other. They couldn't run to the stairway because the man stood right in their way. *What was going to happen now?* both boys wondered.

CHAPTER ELEVEN

Emery found his voice first and blurted out, "Are you going to chop us into pieces and eat us and hide the left-over parts where no one will ever find them?"

The shaggy man made a 'yuck' face and said, "No, thank you. I've already eaten." He pointed back at a crumpled bag tossed near where he slept. The two boys recognized it right away. McDonald's. Somehow knowing the man ate hamburgers and French fries made him seem less like a monster to them.

"Well," the man said. "Since none of us are supposed to be here, why don't we introduce ourselves and explain why we are?"

Philip felt his heart slowing down. When he'd first seen the man, it felt like an electric shock went through him. What a stupid question Emery had asked. Chop them into pieces and eat them. Philip hurried to respond before Emery told the man why they were really in the house.

"We were... exploring. You know. This empty house. And... and... It seemed like fun. A neat place to hide or have a secret clubhouse."

"Ah, same as me. Why don't you both sit down?" The man turned back to his spot under the staircase and sat on the thin mattress.

The boys didn't move. They looked at each other. They knew, with the man seated, they could bolt for the stairway and get out of the house before he could catch them, but things didn't seem so scary now. Philip bravely took a step forward and lowered himself to the ground. Emery followed suit.

"I don't have a real place to live," said the man. "I been sleeping outside all summer, but with the chilly weather I found this empty house, and it seemed like the thing to do. At least until someone kicked me out."

"What's your name?" Emery asked.

"Walter," the man answered. "Walter the derelict." The man laughed. "Life can take some funny turns, boys. And who are you?"

"Philip, the student."

"Emery, the student, too."

"Hello, Philip. Hello, Emery, students both. As I said, with no place to go, I came here. You're the two young fellows who cut the lawn, aren't you?"

"You saw us? You were here then?" Philip asked in some surprise.

"Yep."

"Did you open the window while we were working?" asked Emery. Philip had been thinking the same question.

"I did. How did you know?"

Philip explained.

"Very observant of you. I love the smell of new cut grass. Don't you? So I opened the window and lay down underneath it on the floor breathing it in. It's about the most expensive entertainment I can afford these days."

"Don't you have a job?" Emery asked.

"Had one. Lost it. Not my fault," he said with emphasis, as if having the boys understand that fact was important to him. "Can't find another. Been over a year now, and so no money means no apartment. The government gives me some, but it's not enough for me to keep living where I used to live. So I'm trying to save up to get a new start, but..." He moved both his hands. "It takes a while." He looked straight at the boys, one of the few times he had. "Boys, I have to ask you a favor. If people know I'm here, they're going to ask me to leave or maybe arrest me, even though I'm not hurting anything. You think you could keep me a secret? If you want to come back in and use this place as a clubhouse or something, it's all right with me. I'll be glad for the company."

"Does anyone else beside you ever come in this house?" Philip asked. He tapped Emery's knee, and Emery knew Philip was really asking about the robbers and the loot.

Walter shook his head. "Nope. And I hope no one does. Would scare me to death if anyone did. You two scared the dickens out of me today. Good thing I was asleep when you were creeping around. You'd probably've given me a heart attack."

"Did you take our sandwiches off the porch the day we cut the grass?" Philip asked.

"Guilty," Walter answered.

"And another one the next day?" Emery asked.

"Guilty again."

"And did you take a sandwich from my lunch when I left my book bag in front of Emery's house?" Philip asked.

"Was that yours? Guilty a third time. Sometimes it's hard to get enough food, but I'll pay you back, boys. Soon as I get back on my feet again."

Emery and Philip exchanged a glance, and Philip said, "We believe you."

No one spoke until Philip said, "Well, I guess me and Emery better go."

Walter looked at them. "Well, it was darn nice to meet you. I hope we didn't scare each other too much. Come back again if you want, though I suppose I shouldn't tell you to do that. It's probably wrong. But, well..." He shrugged. "I get lonely."

The two boys rose but Walter did not.

"You boys take care. Better not let anyone see you leave."

"How do you get in here?" Emery asked.

"I broke the little window in the back door, and now I reach inside for the knob."

"Same as I did," said Emery.

"You're a smart boy." Walter laughed. "Maybe you'll make a good derelict someday. Get out safe now. Be careful."

The boys promised they would be and, after saying goodbye to Walter, they went upstairs and snuck out the back door. They hurried straight for Emery's house. His mother would be busy with his two little sisters, and they could talk in private. And they had a *lot* to talk about.

CHAPTER TWELVE

Philip and Emery found the prospect of having a secret, no-longer-haunted, clubhouse complete with a mysterious man in it too exciting for them to tell anyone and spoil it. Right after school the next two days they dropped their books at one of their houses and made their slow and secret way to what they still called the haunted house. They took Walter some food they snuck out of their own kitchens and sat and talked or mostly listened to him as he told them the story of his life. On Thursday, Emery complained about some homework the boys had, and Walter told them they should bring their tough homework with them next time. He'd be happy to help them out with it. But since they rarely got homework on Fridays, their next homework wouldn't be till Monday, four days away.

That night Philip's father walked in the door after work and called Philip's name. Philip rolled off his bed—he'd gotten home from the haunted house moments earlier—and went downstairs to meet his father.

"Hi, Dad."

"How are you, Flipster?"

"Good."

"I got a phone call today about you."

Philip felt goose bumps run up his arm. Had someone seen him going into the haunted house? "About what?" he asked trying not to sound nervous.

"The real estate agent called praising what a good job you did fixing up the lawn on the house around the corner. He said he'd be happy if you could go around to every house he's trying to sell and fix it up. He's finally getting some calls about it."

About *it*? The haunted house? "You mean someone's going to *buy* the house?" Philip asked, again trying to maintain a normal tone of voice, even though he got more nervous with each passing sentence his father spoke.

"Well, not yet, but he'll be taking some people to see the house tomorrow morning."

"Tomorrow morning?"

Philip's father gave him a funny look. "Yes, tomorrow morning. Why?"

"Oh, no reason. I guess I'm used to the house being empty is all."

Philip's mother walked into the living room, and Philip's father greeted her. "Hi, honey. What's for dinner?"

Philip tuned out the rest of the conversation and took himself back up to his bedroom. People were visiting the haunted house tomorrow morning. He had to warn Walter. If they caught Walter in the house, who knows what would happen to him? He said he could be arrested and put into jail. Even if he didn't get arrested, he'd get chased out and have no place to live, and it was getting colder every day.

Philip looked out the window into the dark evening. He'd never be allowed out of the house this late, but he had to find some way to warn Walter nonetheless.

"Dinner, Philip," he heard his mother call.

Dinner. Six o'clock already, and he had to go to bed at nine-thirty. He didn't have much time. Maybe Emery... no, Emery wouldn't be able to help. He'd heard Emery tell Walter he was going over his aunt's house tonight. Philip knew he'd never be home in time and couldn't get out of the house even if he got home in time. He couldn't even phone Emery to talk things over. The best he could do was to go and get Emery extra early next morning before school.

"Philip, while it's hot. Let's go," came his father's voice.

Philip rolled off the bed and started downstairs to dinner. This was a tough problem to find an answer to, but he'd always managed to come up with something before whenever he got into trouble. He sure hoped he could come up with something this time.

Early next morning Philip put his finger to his lips as he led the way into the haunted house. "Shhh, follow me," he said.

He led the way through the kitchen to the basement door. He opened it.

"Walter? Walter, are you there?"

A voice came from the dark basement. "Yes, I'm here. Philip?"

Philip hit the light switch and waved his hand to go forward. Down the steps he went and turned to where he knew Walter would be lying. Walter was on his knees climbing out from under the staircase. He stood up and his eyes opened wide when he saw the two people standing before him.

"Walter," said Philip, swallowing hard, "I'd like you to meet my Dad."

CHAPTER THIRTEEN

"And then what happened?" Emery asked.

"Well, Walter looked... shocked; even sad. Like I did something wrong to him."

"He probably thought you were trying to get him kicked out of the house."

It was Friday morning, and the two boys walked to school as Philip brought Emery up-to-date.

"But I wasn't."

"Why didn't you tell me before you went there?"

"Last night you were over your aunt's, and I had to do something before the real estate agent took strangers in the house. I didn't know how early the agent guy would show up today. I thought about calling you this morning, but then I thought we might not have enough time before school started, so I set my alarm and got up at *seven* o'clock, woke up my dad, and talked him into going to the haunted house."

"So what happened when your father saw Walter?"

"He started talking to him. He told Walter not to worry. He told him I said nice things about him."

"Was your father mad we snuck in the house?"

"Well, that sort of got pushed out of the way because of Walter."

"Man, just when we find a great place... but w*hat happened?*"

"So my dad invited him to our house."

"To your house! Inside? Is he there now?"

"Yeah."

"What's your father gonna do?"

"I don't know."

"You don't know!"

"No. My father chased me out and told me to go to school."

"Boy, I'd love to know what's happening to Walter. I like him."

"Me, too. My dad'll probably tell me tonight."

"When he does, call me right away."

"Don't worry. I will."

"So did he tell you yet?" were Emery's first words. He rushed to Philip's house as soon as he could Saturday morning.

Philip's glum face told him the answer. "No. Nothing last night and he already went out this morning."

"No! How could he not tell you? What did he say? Did you ask him?"

"Yes, I asked him. Of course I asked him. Ten times I asked him. He only said Walter was being taken care of."

"Did he say it... how did he say it? 'Taken care of.' He didn't mean he'd get punished, did he? Like in jail."

"No, I don't think so. My dad smiled kind of funny."

Emery looked confused.

Philip shrugged. "Like he made a joke or was hiding something."

Emery slumped into one corner of his sofa. Philip slumped into the other corner.

"Grownups never tell you anything," Emery grumbled. "You think your dad will tell you anything *today*?"

Philip shrugged. "I hope so. He better. I'll ask."

They stayed silent for a while.

"What do you want to do?" Emery asked.

"I don't know."

"At least we already finished our stupid project," Emery said. "I'll bet everyone else in class is working on it like crazy this weekend."

"Mr. Ware said we could improve it."

"It's improved enough already," said Emery. "I don't want to think about it anymore. Want to watch one of those movies your dad bought?"

"You mean one of those Abbott and Costello movies? Yeah, okay. We liked the one about Frankenstein and Dracula he made us watch."

"Good. They're pretty funny," Emery agreed.

"I'll get the movies. They're upstairs."

Despite pestering his father for two days for news about Walter, Philip had nothing to share with Emery on either Saturday or Sunday, and the first thing Emery said on Monday morning as he and Philip walked to school was, "So, did your dad tell you anything *yet?* He must have told you something by now, right?"

"No! He won't tell me *anything!* He gives me a funny smile and says not to worry about it. It's really making me mad. I asked him so many times he sent me to my bedroom at eight o'clock last night."

"That's mean, not telling us what happened to Walter. We have a right to know, don't we?"

"Nobody thinks so but me and you."

"Oh, well. At least we have an easy day today. We already reported on our beautification project."

"I want to know what happened to Walter," Philip said defiantly.

"Me, too," Emery agreed, and the boys kept walking.

They reached school and their day began the same as ever; reading, math, and gym. At lunch they stood in the warmest spot they could find in the schoolyard and discussed Walter, and after lunch the class prepared to report on their projects. Philip and Emery slumped down in their seats, their consciences clear, their work done, content to see their classmates suffer through their reports.

As Mr. Ware announced that Kevin would report on his project first, Mr. Greif, the principal, walked into the classroom.

"Afternoon, Mr. Ware. I understand your class is giving their 'Neighborhood Service' reports this afternoon."

"That's right." The class could see the principal's visit puzzled Mr. Ware. "Something has come to my attention. Something your class has done during this project that deserves to be recognized."

Everyone in the class immediately thought of their classmate Wilson, the super-student. Everything he did seemed to deserve special attention, and they all wondered what he'd done now.

The principal gestured to the classroom door. Philip and Emery bolted upright in their seats as Walter walked into the room.

He looked different—a lot cleaner; his hair and beard were neat and even; he even wore new-looking clothes.

"This is Walter Benson," Mr. Greif said. "Walter is going to tell you his story."

Walter cleared his throat. He looked at Philip and Emery and smiled.

"I'm sure you know who Philip and Emery are, your classmates."

Everyone's head turned toward the two boys who sat next to each other. They didn't know whether to be embarrassed or thrilled by the attention.

Walter told the story of how he met the two boys.

Philip and Emery could feel the excitement in the class as everyone learned how they'd snuck into the empty house and befriended Walter.

"I've had an awful lot of bad luck," Walter continued. "I won't bother you with all that, but I had no home, not much money, not much food, not much... hope. These two boys, your friends, figured out a way to give all of that back to me. Philip's dad talked to me and finally put me in touch with the real estate agent responsible for the house I mentioned. Seems he'd always wanted someone who could take care of the different houses he was trying to sell. Fix them up. Or, as the boys did, keep the lawn neat and presentable. Now that job belongs to me. He gave it to me, and I'm going to work hard at it. Plus, the real estate agent knows a woman who wants to rent a tiny apartment above her garage. It's not very big, but it's enough for me, and with my new job, I can afford it." He moved his gaze to the two boys. "Philip and Emery, you're welcome there any time."

"Well, Mr. Benson, you've told us quite a story," said Mr. Greif. He turned to face the class. "Philip, Emery, I don't think I've ever been prouder of any students from our school than I am of you both at this moment, and you should be proud of yourselves. Mr. Ware, what do you think? A+ for helping the neighborhood?"

"A++, Mr. Greif. Their original project was good. But this... it's terrific. Way to go, guys." Mr. Ware gave them a thumbs-up.

Walter waved to them as the principal led him from the classroom, and Philip and Emery spent a very pleasant afternoon basking in the unspoken but very noticeable admiration of their classmates.

CHAPTER FOURTEEN

Philip pounced on his father the moment he returned home from work. "Dad, you didn't tell me anything. How did Walter get a job? How did he end up at school today?"

"Whoa, whoa. Slow down." Philip watched his father hang his coat in the hall closet. "Come, come," his father said, waving him into the living room. "Now, one question at a time."

"How did Walter end up in my classroom this afternoon? And what happened to him over the weekend?"

"That's two questions, but you were right. Walter seemed like a very nice fellow. So when I bundled you off to school on Friday, I got him to tell me a little of his history. He used to work over in McClaron's, the big department store that went out of business."

"Wow! So how'd he end up living in an empty house?"

"When the store closed down, the company that took it over didn't offer him another job, and afterwards he simply had a long string of bad luck. So, I thought of Mr. Schilling, the real estate agent."

"I know who you mean." The drudgery of lawn mowing filled Philip's mind for a moment.

"Well, I thought since he jokingly said he'd like to hire you to keep the houses he sold in good order, he might seriously consider hiring Walter. So on my way to work on Friday, I took Walter to meet him, and Walter told his story to Mr. Schilling, but Mr. Schilling checked out the facts."

"What facts?"

"Oh, about whether Walter really worked at McClaron's or not. Was he a good worker? Some other stuff. Finally, Mr. Schilling called me and said everything checked out. Walter, it seems, is a truthful man."

"I told you he was okay."

"I remembered your telling me your class did their reports this afternoon, so I called Mr. Greif, told him the story, and he agreed you and Emery deserved some recognition for what you did for Walter."

"But I didn't do anything. All I did was tell you about him."

"Well, you wanted to keep Walter out of trouble, didn't you? You could have told Walter to avoid the house for a while and not told me. It seems *you're* an honest fellow, too, Flipster. I hope you weren't too embarrassed today. Walter called me and told me how it went. He said you and Emery were blushing."

"We were really surprised. Mr. Greif waved his hand at the door, and Walter appeared like magic."

"So, anyway, let me go say hello to your mother."

"Dad, can I run down to Emery's. He's been asking me every day what happened to Walter."

Mr. Felton glanced at his watch. "Okay, be back by dinner, though, or your mother will start singing to you."

"I will. Oh, Walter said he was getting some apartment over some garage, and we were invited anytime we wanted. Where is it?"

"Two blocks over. Horrocks Street."

"Wow, so close."

"Don't make a nuisance of yourself. And don't forget. Walter will be busy working at his new job." Mr. Felton smiled.

Philip smiled back.

"Oh, Dad. Did they ever catch those robbers?"

"Not that I know."

The loot hasn't been found yet, Philip thought. *It's still out there.*

"One other thing," Mr. Felton said. The smile left his face. "There will be no more traipsing about in empty, abandoned houses. At all. Understand?"

Philip had been waiting for that. He nodded.

"Good. Then this will all have a happy ending. Be back in time for dinner."

Philip rushed for his jacket and charged out the door. He couldn't wait to tell Emery the rest of Walter's story and remind him about the missing loot—still out there someplace waiting to be found—maybe even by them!

Philip and the Monsters
DEDICATION

To Princess Taryn

CHAPTER ONE

"Boo!" shouted Emery. Philip's heart shot up, and his stomach tumbled. He spun to face his friend.

"Are you crazy? Are you really crazy? Why did you do that? I walk into your house and you jump out like a maniac? You almost gave me a heart attack."

Emery laughed and waved a hand at Philip. "Get out. We're too young to have heart attacks. Unless," said Emery in a spooky voice, "your arteries are clogged with the cholesterol of fear."

Philip stared at Emery.

"What?" Emery asked.

Philip continued to stare.

Emery smiled nervously and shrugged.

Philip didn't move a muscle.

Emery blinked and blinked again.

Philip continued to stare and refused to blink.

"Say something, please," said Emery in a small voice. He waited. Philip said nothing. "Come on, you're scaring me."

Philip kept on staring and counted to himself. When he reached three, he threw his arms in the air and shouted, "BOOOO!"

"Ahhh!" Emery burst out. "Why did you do that? Are you crazy, too? You were scaring me and then you scared me. Why'd you scare me?"

"Can we go back to the beginning?" Philip asked slowly, still giving Emery his coldest stare.

"The beginning?"

"Did you ask me to come over so we could do our homework together?"

"Yes, I did," said Emery, paying very close attention to Philip's questions. He didn't want Philip to start staring and BOO-ing him again.

"Did you tell me you would leave the front door open, and I should just walk in?"

"Yes, I did."

"Why?"

"So I could jump out and scare you."

"Then you admit it!" Philip cried. He tried to stay calm. "Why did you want to scare me?"

"Uh, because you *said* I could."

Philip stared at Emery again.

"Are you going to do the staring *Boo!* thing again, because... ?" Emery stepped back, arms out, hands waving slowly.

"No, stand still," Philip said softly. "When did I say you could jump out at me and try to give me a heart attack? When? When did I say it?"

"You said we would do our homework together, didn't you?"

"Yeah, so? Is giving me a heart attack doing our homework together?" Philip shouted.

"No, but scaring you is. I'm doing my report on how people act when they get scared. You have to do a report too, you know. The class report we have to do about a feeling. Remember?"

"What was the stuff you said before?"

"Before? When?"

"Before. About the arteries and the clogging."

Emery laughed. "Did you like it? I made it up. I read this newspaper article about good heart health, and I read a different article about how peoples' hearts beat faster when they get scared."

"You didn't have to read about it. I could have told you."

"Yeah well, I put the two things together and I said..."

"I know what you said. What does cholesterol have to do with your report?"

"Nothing. I made a joke, for Pete's sake."

"Some dumb joke. Next time, save it for Pete."

"Never mind the joke. Tell me what you felt when you got scared." Emery scrambled to the floor and lay on his stomach, pencil in hand and notebook open. "Go on."

Philip tried the best he could to remember everything he felt when Emery jumped out at him. As Philip talked, Emery wrote fast.

"Good," said Emery, his pencil zipping across the paper. "Good. Now let me write what I felt when you scared me."

When Emery finished writing, Philip said, "Lemme see." Emery handed him the notebook.

Philip read, "When Philip first scared me by staring, I got scared because I didn't know what he was doing. I felt scared because I didn't know what would happen next. When Philip jumped at me, I felt really scared, heart-beating scared."

Philip looked at Emery, impressed. "Pretty neat. You got scared a different way each time."

"Yeah, it's great for my report. Now I need you to add things to my list."

"What list?"

"My list of things people get scared by. Tell me what things scare you. You know, to see or think about. Know what my mother said? She said hairy people scare her. You know with hairy hands and arms and eyebrows and nose hairs and hair where it shouldn't be, like on warts and stuff."

"Disgusting!"

"Yeah, but scary. Go on, what scares you?"

"What did you put for yourself?"

Emery flipped back a few pages. "I put waking up in the dark in a strange place." Philip agreed. No argument there. It happened to him. "Watching scary movies in the dark when my parents are out." Philip agreed again. Still no argument. "Being alone in the house. Sometimes. Like at night. That's all."

"They're all good ones."

"Your turn."

"You took all the good ones."

"You have to give me something different. Come on."

"The haunted house scared us. Going inside it, remember?"

Emery wrote it down.

"Somebody finally moved in there, you know," Emery said, when he finished writing.

"I heard. My dad told me. At least we won't have to mow their lawn anymore. The new people can mow their own lawn." He and Emery had beautified the deserted house by mowing its lawn as part of a community service project.

"Give me one more. A good one. How about monsters? Are you afraid of monsters?"

"What kind of monsters?"

"Regular monsters. You know. Frankenstein, Dracula, Wolfman."

"Everybody's supposed to be afraid of them, but they're not real."

"I'll put it anyway."

"Under my name?"

"Sure."

"No, no," Philip scoffed. "I don't want everybody in the class to think I'm afraid of Dracula. Put your cousin Leon's name instead of mine. He's afraid of everything."

"All right. All right. So there. Only one more person to interview and I'm done making a list. I'll ask Mrs. Moriarty later what she's scared of." Mrs. Moriarty was their favorite neighbor. "Fourth grade projects aren't so bad. You pick yours yet?" Emery closed his notebook and tossed it on the sofa.

"No," said Philip.

"You better hurry up. Want to go see what the new haunted house family looks like?"

Philip looked out the window. It was early December and darkness arrived early. Philip checked his watch, hoping Emery got the message and would suggest a time with more daylight available.

"We're allowed out till five," Emery argued.

"Let's go tomorrow right after school." Philip thought of the bright afternoon sunshine. "We'll have more time."

"Okay," Emery agreed. "You afraid to walk home alone? Want me to walk you?"

"No! My arteries are not clogged with the cholesterol of fear."

The two boys laughed. Philip gathered up his coat from the floor where he'd dropped it and hurried home alone, as fast as he could.

CHAPTER TWO

"Are you scared?" Emery asked softly as they walked down the side of Pratt Street opposite the haunted house.

Philip stopped. Emery took two steps and turned around.

"Scared of what?" Philip asked. "Why should I be scared? Are you still doing your project?"

"It's no fun visiting a haunted house if you're not scared, so get scared. And don't talk in a regular voice. Whisper."

"I don't *want* to whisper, and I don't *want* to get scared. We were scared the last time when we went inside, but the house doesn't look haunted anymore. People live in it."

"Suppose a family of monsters moved into the house."

Philip rolled his eyes. "You mean people with two heads and long tails?"

"No, what about if they're a family of werewolves or vampires?"

Philip's voice rose. "Why would werewolves or vampires move into our neighborhood?"

"It's the perfect place. Nobody would suspect them?"

"You would."

"I *do*. I suspect everyone. I should never have made scariness my project. Now everything scares me."

"I still didn't pick a feeling yet for my report. Such a stupid project. Who can do a project on a feeling people have?" Philip didn't want to admit Emery's project made him jealous. He'd picked a good topic and a fun one besides.

The boys started down the street again. "Let's cross," said Emery.

As they crossed the street, Emery touched Philip's shoulder and pointed up. A huge black cloud which sat over the schoolyard at dismissal had gotten darker and covered up more and more of the sky. "The closer we get to the haunted house," Emery whispered, "the darker it gets."

Philip had noticed, but he refused to mention it—although it did seem to be a funny coincidence. They walked slower and slower as they got near the house.

Suddenly, Emery burst out, "Yipe! Look, they put out a new mailbox." On the edge of the sidewalk near the street a wooden stake driven down into the grass held the mailbox. Emery and Philip stepped into the street to face it and take a better look.

The black mailbox had a white door, decorated with painted buttons to look like the front of a man's white shirt. The mailbox itself looked like a black coat or cape. Attached to the top of the mailbox loomed the wooden face of a vampire, red-dripping teeth, shiny straight-back black hair, and evil eyes looking down to see what the mailman slipped into the mailbox. The boys studied the mailbox and turned to one another.

"I never saw a mailbox like this before?" Philip asked softly.

"*Now* you're whispering. Are you scared?"

"No, but it's a weird mailbox, don't you think?"

"Maybe like a dentist hangs a tooth outside his office, they hang this up to show what they do."

"What who do?"

"Who do? You mean voodoo?"

"No, I don't mean voodoo," Philip said loudly. "I mean what who do. Who are you talking about?"

"Vampires. Maybe it's like an advertisement."

"Advertisement? An advertisement for what?"

"To drink blood. You know, come in and have your veins drained."

Philip stared at Emery.

"You're staring again," Emery mumbled.

"An advertisement for people to have their veins drained? Like there's gonna be a long line of people who want their..." Philip stopped. Looking at the mailbox straight on from the street had not allowed the two boys to read the names painted on the side, but as they moved onto the sidewalk, Philip's eyes fell on the painted name.

"Uh oh," Philip said, eyes widening.

"What?" Emery cried.

"Oh, nothing. Their name. Whew! I thought it said the *Monster* family."

"Where?"

"There, on the side."

Emery studied the name and spelled it out loud. "M-o-s-t-e-r/T-a-l-b-o-t. It almost spells *monster.*"

"At least Talbot's a regular name."

A drop of rain fell, and as Philip glanced toward the sky, he saw something in the upstairs window of the house. "Look. Look up there!" he cried in alarm.

"Where? Look where?" Emery spun around until Philip grabbed him by the shoulders and aimed him.

"Look up."

"Okay, I'm looking up, but I don't see anything. What was it?"

"I don't know. There. There it is again. You see it now, don't you?"

"I see it! I see it!" Something black flitted behind the white shade covering the brightly lit upstairs window.

"It looked like..." Emery began."

"Don't say it," Philip interrupted.

"A bat," Emery finished.

"I *told* you not to say it." Philip took a moment to ponder. "Why would a bat be flying around in the house?"

"Could be they have strange pets."

"I don't think so."

"Maybe it's wild and got in the house, and they're trying to chase it out."

"I don't think so," said Philip. "Uh oh!"

The shade on the upstairs window rose slowly. A dark figure appeared at the window as the first rumble of thunder from the coming storm rolled through the darkening afternoon. The figure at the window looked directly down at them. Suddenly, the light in the room went out, and darkness swallowed the figure.

"You don't think it could have turned into a..."

"Don't say it," Philip interrupted.

Emery flicked his thumb over his shoulder in the direction of the mailbox and whispered, "Vamp..."

"*Argh!* I told you not to say it. Stop saying things I tell you not to say."

Emery tapped the head of the vampire on the mailbox.

Another burst of thunder, much louder than the first, crashed across the sky.

"I read vampires can create storms and stuff," said Emery in a low voice, stepping closer to Philip.

"Listen!" Philip cried as a sharp howl broke the silence. "Mrs. Wenner's dog, probably. Maybe it doesn't like the thunder."

"You *sure* it's her dog? It sounded like a w..."

"Don't say it," Philip insisted.

Emery couldn't help himself. "A wolf," he cried. "Maybe a werewolf."

"I *told* you not to say it."

"So, I said it. So what?"

"Never mind. Let's get out of here. I hate this house, and I'm tired of whispering."

A small truck pulled to a stop in front of the Moster/Talbot house, and Philip and Emery moved behind a tree. Emery poked his head out one side of the tree; Philip poked his head out the other side. Two men in overalls got out and went around to the back of the truck.

"Hurry up before it really starts coming down," one man said to the other.

They quickly opened the rear doors of the truck and pulled out a long rectangular box made of wood. The boys noticed small, round holes punched into the side of the box. The box had wheels, and the men rolled the box along and lifted it up onto the porch. One man rang the doorbell.

"Emery, you can see better. Tell me who answers." Emery leaned out from the tree.

"Somebody opened the door. I can't see who. It's too dark." Emery stepped out further from the tree, but Philip pulled him back.

"Don't. It'll see you," said Philip.

Emery ducked back behind the tree. "It? It? What it? You saw an it? Did you see an it?"

Philip shushed him, and the two boys watched the men push the box through the doorway. A moment later the men left the house, climbed back into their truck, and drove away.

The two boys bustled away from the house toward the safety of home. "What do you think they had in the box?" Emery asked.

"I don't..." Suddenly, Philip thought of the long box and the name on the mailbox at the same time. "Moster/Talbot."

"Moster/Talbot what?"

"Remember the movie we saw? The one my dad made us watch from one of those sets he buys? The name! The box!"

"What movie? What name? What box?"

"Talbot. Talbot," Philip insisted. "Let's go to my house. You can call your mom and ask to eat over. I'll ask my dad to let us watch the movie again."

"What movie? What movie?"

"Stop asking so many questions and come on."

The rain began to fall hard, and as the two boys ran down the street, Emery tried hard to remember what movie Philip meant.

CHAPTER THREE

"I can't stay to watch the whole movie," said Emery after Philip told him which movie he meant.

"Why? Scared to?"

"No," Emery snapped. "I got homework to do."

"You don't have to watch the whole movie. The beginning's enough. I don't know why you don't remember things."

"I remember things. I just don't remember what I'm supposed to remember about this movie."

"Think back over everything we did after school and find something in the movie to match it."

Emery thought back. "I can't remember anything special. We talked about monsters, and the movie has monsters in it, but so what?"

"We *talked* about monsters? Only talked? You watch and you'll see so what."

Philip hit the play button on the DVD player, and the movie began. The title read:

Abbott and Costello Meet Frankenstein

The two boys watched as a short, monster-filled cartoon ran behind the movie's credits.

"It's not scary yet," said Emery. "I like cartoons."

Then the movie started.

"Okay, now maybe it's a *little* scary," said Emery. "But today wasn't foggy or..."

"Shh. Watch."

A dark, foggy London night long ago. The blinds on a hotel window open, and a frightened man peers nervously out. He hurries to the telephone to see whether his phone call to America has been completed. It hasn't and he tells the oper-

ator to hurry. *Two silly guys, one tall, Chick Young, and the other short and chubby, Wilbur Gray, run the baggage room of a train station somewhere in America. After Wilbur pulls out the bottom suitcase from a high pile and knocks everything else off the cart, their phone rings. It's a long-distance call from the frightened man in the London hotel room.*

"Hello. Do you have two crates addressed to the Mac-Dougal House of Horrors?"

"What's the number on the checks?" asks chubby Wilbur.

"Never mind that. Tonight the moon will be full here. I haven't much time. Now listen closely. I'm flying out of here at dawn. Under no circumstances are you to deliver those crates until I arrive. Understand? Under..."

The man stops talking and begins to growl. We see his face change, and he becomes a werewolf!

Wilbur tells the man to stop gargling into the phone because he can't understand him. Then Wilbur tells him to get his dog away from the phone, but the werewolf goes wild and disappears.

Chick and Wilbur deliver the two crates to MacDougal's House of Horrors and out of the two crates come Dracula and the Frankenstein monster. While Chick is outside, Dracula hypnotizes Wilbur, but Wilbur awakens and sees the two monsters sneak off. He and Chick get arrested and put in jail for stealing whatever was in the now empty crates. No one believes Wilbur when he tells the truth about what he saw.

Finally out of jail, they're back in their hotel room when the Wolfman from London, back again in human form, walks down their hallway looking at the numbers on the hotel doors. He knocks on theirs.

Wilbur opens the door.

The Wolfman says, "You're Wilbur Gray."

Wilbur says, "Yes, sir."

"Then you must be Chick Young."

"So what?" says Chick.

"I'm Lawrence Talbot. I've been looking all over town for you."

Philip stopped the movie, and the two boys turned and faced one another.

"Did he say Talbot?" Emery whispered.

"Yes! Talbot! The same name, and we saw them get a long box delivered."

"Put the lights on," said Emery. "Put 'em on!"

Philip leaned over and turned on the table lamp next to the sofa where they sat.

"Lawrence Talbot," Emery whispered.

"It's the same name," Philip repeated.

"You don't think... you don't think... in the box..."

"A monster? A Frankenstein monster? No. I don't know. I don't think so. A whole big monster couldn't fit in such a little box."

"A baby Frankenstein! It could be a baby Frankenstein! A baby Frankenstein would fit."

The boys eyes met again and Emery said, "A bat upstairs; a baby Frankenstein in a box; and Lawrence Talbot. A vampire, a monster and a werewolf living almost right next door to us."

"I have a calendar in the kitchen," said Philip, jumping up from the sofa. "Let's go check it."

"Why? You want to see how many days we have left to live?"

"No, we have to check the date of the next full moon."

Shoulder-to-shoulder both boys went into the kitchen where a big calendar with a picture of a Christmas tree hung next to the refrigerator. Philip ran his finger over it and said, "Today is Tuesday. The full moon is this Friday."

"Oh," moaned Emery. "We might not last till this Friday. What are we going to do?"

"You have to get your mom to invite me to sleep over on Friday."

"Why?"

"We have to watch that house. You can see it from your bedroom, right?

"Some of it."

The phone rang.

"Ahhh!" Both boys jumped.

Philip's mother's voice came from upstairs. "It's your mother, Emery. You have to go now."

Emery gathered up his coat and school bag. "When we watch the house, what'll we look for?"

"Those three—things—you just said before, but don't say them again. Remember," whispered Philip as his father joined them at the front door. "Sleepover, tell your mother."

"You want to walk me home?"

Philip shook his head rapidly.

"I'll walk you," said Philip's father.

"See you," said Emery, greatly relieved.

Philip waved goodbye. He ran to the dining room window and watched until he saw his father coming safely back up the pathway to their front door. You never knew what might happen with neighbors like they had.

CHAPTER FOUR

It began snowing Thursday afternoon. The children in Philip's classroom oohed and aahed their approval of the change in the weather right in the middle of Mr. Ware's math lesson. The noises didn't make him happy, but he understood, so he switched over to a lesson on the formation of snow and left common denominators for another time.

Philip played with Emery in the falling snow after school and came home cold, wet, and happy. He changed into dry clothing and lay down on his bed to rest a minute and think.

Philip had spent much of today and the day before in deep discussions with Emery over whether a genuine monster could really exist. At first they concluded no; monsters only lived in fairy tales. But after talking it over further, they concluded yes. Why would people write about monsters and make so many movies about something make-believe? They realized there could be lots of weird and different things going on in faraway places they didn't know anything about. Even if monsters did exist in the world, though, they concluded *they* were safe because a monster could never show up right in their own neighborhood. Impossible! After more discussion they concluded they weren't safe at all because if monsters existed, every one of them had to be *somewhere,* so why *not* their neighborhood as well as any other? Philip pointed out the Talbot name on the mailbox and the howling of what might or might not have been Mrs. Wenner's dog. Emery threw in the fluttering of the bat in the upstairs window of the Moster/Talbot house and the air holes in the baby Frankenstein box. When time for discussing things ran out, the boys absolutely positively concluded that maybe these monsters might exist, and they could even be right in their own neighborhood, as impossible as it seemed. Yes, of that much they were certain.

Philip father's called from downstairs so Philip went to see what he wanted.

"What are you doing home so soon?" Philip asked. "It's only five o'clock."

"I decided to leave the office before the snow got too bad to drive in. It's supposed to stop before midnight. Probably not enough to cancel school, I'm afraid."

"Tomorrow's Friday anyway," said Philip. "Last day. And we have gym."

"I bought a couple new movies—new old movies. This one's for you. Here. You and Emery liked the Frankenstein and werewolf movie so much, I'm sure you'll like this one."

Philip reluctantly took the plastic bag his father handed him and pulled out a DVD with a picture of a werewolf under the title of the movie.

The Wolfman

The cover showed the face and shoulders of a hairy-headed, big-nosed werewolf with his lower teeth jutting out of his partly opened mouth. Over the werewolf's right shoulder a smaller picture showed him holding onto a woman falling over backwards in his arms. Someone he planned to snack on later, Philip guessed. Fog covered the ground behind the werewolf's head and a black sky loomed overhead. As Philip inspected the pictures on the box, he realized this werewolf looked like the werewolf in the first movie. He turned the DVD case over and recognized the name. Lon Chaney, Jr. The same name as in the first movie.

After dinner Philip's mom and dad took their movie upstairs to watch. Philip looked at *The Wolfman* DVD case on the coffee table in the living room and decided he'd wait until tomorrow and watch it with Emery. The phone rang.

Philip ran to the kitchen and grabbed the receiver. "Hello."

"Philip!"

"I got it, Mom. It's Emery." Philip waited for his mother to hang up. "What do you want, Emery?"

"Philip, he's here. He's here!"

"Who's here? Where are you?

"Larry Talbot. He's here! Right in my house."

"Larry Talbot. The Wolfman? What are you talking about? You mean a movie?"

"No, no, no. No movie. He's here. He's really here. He's the guy who moved into in the haunted house! My mother knows him, and he's right downstairs, and his last name's Talbot. Larry Talbot. I gotta go. Pray for me." The phone went dead.

Pray for him! Emery had never said anything like that before. Philip spent an uneasy night worrying about his friend, and felt greatly relieved to see Emery waiting on the sidewalk the next morning making designs in the snow with the toe of his snow boot. He ran up to him.

"What were you talking about? Larry Talbot visited your house?"

As they walked toward school, Emery explained. "My mother went to high school or something with him. He's even got a wife and a kid. A little kid. He knew where my mother lived and stopped in."

"Did his whole family come?"

"No. Only him. Thank goodness he only stayed a few minutes, but when my mother introduced him and said where he lived and told me his name, I almost fainted. I had to shake his hand, and his hand was freezing! He's tall and skinny, and he dressed just like his mailbox. White shirt and black pants. I never want to see him again. He is *so* scary looking, and he didn't smile even once! He looks like one of those guys who buries people and dresses in black all time. And he's got a hairy face, too."

"You mean a beard?"

"It's sort of a beard on his chin, but the rest of his face is just fuzzy hairy like he didn't really start shaving yet."

"So what did he do when he visited?"

"He stayed a little while and talked to my mother and father."

"Did you listen?"

"No, I ran upstairs to call you right away, and I stayed upstairs."

"So," Philip said slowly, "do you think he's a werewolf like we saw in the movie?"

"How do I know? You think he's going to say, 'Hi, I'm a werewolf. May I bite your face off?'"

"No, I guess he wouldn't say that."

"Now he knows where I live. I watched from the top of the stairs, and before he left, guess what he did?"

"What?"

"He went and looked out the window."

Philip stared at Emery in confusion. "What was out the window?"

"The moon."

Philip gasped.

The idea that Larry Talbot thought it important to take a look at the moon, which they both knew would be full that night, silenced both boys.

"You think he had to get home, you know, before... ?" said Philip softly.

"Before he changed?"

Philip nodded.

Emery didn't answer. He didn't have to, since both boys had reached an unspoken agreement. After a moment he said, "I have to go to Mrs. Moriarty's tonight to be baby sat, but we're lucky. Mrs. Moriarty asked if I wanted company, and I said you so she's going to call your mom today and ask if you can eat dinner over. My mom's going to call your mom and see if you can sleep over my house."

"Good. Yesterday, my father brought home a movie for us to watch. He said he thought we'd like it. Ha!"

"What movie?"

"*The Wolfman.*"

"*The Wolfman!* No way!"

"Yes way, and it's got the same guy in it, the Larry Talbot guy."

"The guy from the haunted house is a movie star?" Emery cried, his eyes popping open.

"No, stupid. The guy who's Larry Talbot in the first movie. Same face. Same guy."

"Oooohhhh." The boys stopped talking and looked to their right. The Talbot house sat in the morning sunlight, peaceful and pretty. The snowfall had turned the neighborhood into a Christmas card scene, and this scariest of houses fit right in.

"Looks okay now, doesn't it?" said Emery. "You think we'll see anything tonight when the moon's full?"

"You sound like you think we will."

"I can't help it. This house. Larry Talbot. Everything. It's starting to..." Emery put his hands in front of him and interlaced his fingers.

"Yeah, I know." He had no desire to tease Emery about being scared.

"You think we'll see anything?" Emery repeated.

"This is the full moon night," said Philip, as if that answered the question.

"I know," Emery said in a whisper, as if that concluded the discussion.

They turned their backs on the haunted house and, with only an occasional stop to toss a snowball at a tree, they walked silently the rest of the way to school.

CHAPTER FIVE

"So how are you boys going to entertain yourselves tonight?" Mrs. Moriarty asked. Mrs. Moriarty was Philip's favorite grownup neighbor, and the only grownup he knew who liked candy as much as he did. She always had dishes full of candy right out where you could get at them—she was especially fond of M & Ms—and she never complained if you ate a lot or emptied a dish. She simply filled it up again. She was older than most of his other neighbors, and whenever his or Emery's parents went out, he and Emery always asked for Mrs. Moriarty to do the babysitting.

"We have a movie to watch," said Emery. "Philip's father bought it for him."

"What is it? Would I like it?"

"*The Wolfman*," said Philip. "It's about a werewolf."

"A werewolf! Brrrr! I think I'll pass. Why did your father give you such a scary movie, Philip?"

Philip looked at Emery. "Oh... we... we need to do something for school. Emery's doing a report on scary things."

"Yeah. Remember I interviewed you?"

"Oh, yes. I do. What kind of report are you doing, Philip?"

"Uh, I'm not sure yet."

"They certainly give out different kinds of assignments from when I went to school. I remember once I had to find out the capitals of all the countries in South America. Oh, well. Dinner in fifteen minutes." Mrs. Moriarty disappeared into the kitchen.

Philip motioned Emery to a window in the living room and pulled the curtain aside. The street lamp shone on the now trampled snow. The cars had churned up all the snow in the street, and people had shoveled their sidewalks. Only on people's lawns where no one had walked yet did the snow still appear new-looking.

"I don't see the moon," said Philip.

"Not until seven-fifteen," said Emery.

"So late? You sure?"

"The newspaper said so. I checked."

"Seven-fifteen," Philip repeated. "I guess we're safe until then."

"Did you figure out how we're going to investigate?"

"I think so. How about this? We say we need a schoolbook from my house. I purposely left my math book on the dining room table. We run and get it, and after we have it, we go investigate as long as we can and get back before Mrs. M. gets suspicious."

"Good plan. What time should we... ?"

"Nine. When we're sure the full moon is up."

"Can't we go earlier? Before he... changes?"

"If we go earlier, he won't be a werewolf, and we won't know whether he's a werewolf or not, but if we go when he's *supposed* to be a werewolf and he's not a werewolf, then we proved he's not a werewolf. Don't you see?"

Emery repeated Philip's sentence slowly in his head. "I think so," he agreed doubtfully. "But you left out—suppose we go, and he *is* a werewolf?"

"Dinnertime," came Mrs. Moriarty's voice from the kitchen.

"That's why we gotta watch the movie first. It'll probably tell us things we need to know, like how to get protection against a werewolf."

"Yeah, that might be a good thing to know about."

"Come on, boys," called Mrs. Moriarty again. This time, the boys walked off toward the kitchen.

"This movie's boring," Emery complained. "I thought it would be scary, but it's nothing but a family reunion." He and Philip sat in Mrs. Moriarty's den, lit only by the flickering glow from the television. Mrs. Moriarty watched her own movie in the living room. "It's got a love story, too." Emery frowned. "Yuk! I don't think the girl would like Larry Talbot much if she knew he was busy turning into a werewolf instead of taking her dancing."

"How's she supposed to know that?" Philip responded irritably. "Anyway, he's not a werewolf yet. He's only regular so far. The movie must show how he got to be one. Be quiet and pay attention, will you?"

They watched a while longer, but Emery continued to complain.

"I wish something interesting would happen. He's didn't turn to a Wolfman once yet."

"I told you. He's not one yet. Shhh."

A young woman spoke.

Even a man who is pure in heart
And says his prayers by night
May become a wolf when the wolfbane blooms
And the autumn moon is bright.

"What's wolfbane?" whispered Emery when the woman in the movie finished reciting her poem.

"If it blooms I guess it's a flower," Philip whispered back. "At least it's the winter moon that's bright tonight." He pointed toward the window.

"Wrong. Winter doesn't start till December 21. It's still only autumn."

Sometimes Emery was *too* smart, Philip thought.

"You think we grow wolfbane around here?" Emery asked.

"How do I know? We have to know what it is before we know if we have any or not. Besides, it's cold. No flowers are growing around here. Shhh. They're going to have their fortune told. Watch. Watch."

Larry Talbot and two young women step into the gypsy camp. Larry takes the woman he likes for a walk while the other one goes inside the gypsy wagon to see Bela and his crystal ball. Bela studies what's inside the crystal ball then puts his head in his hands as if he's going to cry. When he looks up at the woman again, he sees a star on the back of her hand. It shimmers a moment, then disappears. He tells her to get out.

"What's the star on her hand mean?" Emery asked in a worried voice. "That guy's seeing things."

"They already said what it means. Pay attention."

"I can't pay attention, it's so boring."

"It's called a pentagram. It means Bela's already a werewolf, and she's going to be his next victim."

"Bela's already a werewolf?" Emery's interesting rose.

"Yeah."

"And the star's a pentagram?"

"Yes, be quiet and listen, will you?"

The woman runs away very frightened. A wolf howls.

"Sounds just like Mrs. Wenner's dog did before," Emery whispered.

Philip shushed him.

The wolf attacks the woman. Larry hears the attack and rushes to the rescue. Using his new walking stick with the silver image of a wolf on the top, he kills the wolf, but before he does, the wolf bites him.

"There. That's how he becomes one," Philip whispered. "An old werewolf bit him."

"Philip..." said Emery.

"Shhh. Watch."

"But, Philip..."

"Shhh!"

There is no wolf body when the police arrive, though, only the body of Bela the gypsy.

A few nights later, the old gypsy woman, Bela's mother, gives Larry a warning as he walks toward home through the gypsy camp.

"You've been a long time coming," she says.

"I'm not buying anything," he says impatiently.

"And I am not selling anything. I expected you sooner."

Larry walks up to the old gypsy woman and says, "Oh, I remember you. That night." He's thinking of the night he fought the wolf.

"Go inside," the woman orders Larry.

He does and she follows.

"You killed a wolf."

"Well, there's no crime in that is there?"

"The wolf was Bela."

"You think I don't know the difference between a wolf and a man?"

"Bela became a wolf, and you killed him. A werewolf can be killed only with a silver bullet or a silver knife or a walking stick with a silver handle."

"You're insane. I tell you I killed a wolf; a plain, ordinary wolf."

"Take this chain, the pentagram. The sign of the wolf. It can break the evil spell."

"Evil spell. Pentagrams. Wolfbane. Ah, I'm sick of the whole thing. I'm gonna get out of here."

The gypsy woman speaks again and Larry stops. She says, "Whoever is bitten by a werewolf and lives becomes a werewolf himself."

"Aw, quit handing me that. You're just wasting your time."

"The wolf bit you, didn't he?"

"Yeah. Yeah, he did."

"Wear this charm over your heart always."

"All right. All right. I'll take it. What's it worth to you?"

"Do you dare to show me the wound?"

"I..."

"Do you dare to show me the wound?"

Larry opens his shirt and shows her.

She says, "Go now and heaven help you."

Philip and Emery moved closer to each other.

Larry meets his girlfriend again.

"Aw, it's only another love scene," Emery moaned.

Larry looks around and says, "Wait listen. Look at the gypsies." The gypsies are scurrying around madly, breaking up their camp.

Finally, Larry asks why. A gypsy says, "There's a werewolf in camp."

Larry's girlfriend runs off and Larry runs home.

"I'm glad his girlfriend ran away," says Emery. "I hope I don't ever see her again. Why do they put love stories in these movies, anyway?"

Larry looks into the mirror in his bedroom. He seems relieved. He takes off his shirt and checks his arms.

"See," said Emery. "He's okay. He's not changing."

"Will you be quiet and watch?"

The two boys moved nearer one another until their elbows touched.

Larry's smile fades. His legs! He feels something funny happening. He falls into a chair and takes off his sock.

"Oh," yelped Emery. "He's all fuzzy. He's got fuzzy legs."

"He's turning. He's turning," spluttered Philip.

Larry takes off his other sock.

"Oh, more fuzz. He's a fuzzy man. He's got fuzz all over. His toes! Look at his toes! Now he's got fuzzy toes!"

The two boys watched in fascination as Larry's feet turned into monstrous, long-toed, hairy claws.

When Larry stands up, both boys see his horrible werewolf face.

"Turn it off," Emery cried. "Turn it off."

Philip rolled off the sofa. "Ow. My arm. Let go of my arm."

"I'm not holding your arm."

"You are, too. I can't turn it off if you won't let me go." Philip peeled Emery's fingers off of his arm and threw himself on his knees in front of the TV set. He pushed buttons until the room got dark and quiet. The blue numerals of the clock on the front of the video player read 9:00.

CHAPTER SIX

Emery peeked into the living room. "Mrs. Moriarty's asleep," he whispered. Mrs. Moriarty, her head back and mouth open, snoozed in front of the television. A toothpaste commercial played as the light from the television danced spookily across her face.

"Maybe we can be back before she even wakes up. Hey, I'm feeling really scared," Emery went on. "This is great. I'll put it in my report. I've got to remember exactly how I feel now."

Philip half hoped Emery would suggest they forget their investigation. It didn't look as if Emery would since he seemed determined to ace his report and actually *liked* being scared. What was there really to be scared of, though? Philip asked himself. A werewolf in the neighborhood. Pssh! Not very likely, but scared or not scared, he knew he couldn't be the one to suggest they not go. Emery would never let him forget it.

Emery kept on. "Go get your math book, just in case. I'm going to make something for us here."

"Make what?" Philip asked.

Mrs. Moriarty made a funny noise. The boys looked into the living room, but she slept on. Emery put his fingers to his lips and shooed Philip.

Philip got his coat from the other room, snuck out the back door, and rushed to his house. He explained his mission to his mother, who complimented him for his and Emery's attention to schoolwork, and rushed back to Mrs. Moriarty's. When he closed the kitchen door behind him, Emery handed him a yardstick with aluminum foil wrapped around the top of it. He had a second one for himself.

Philip took the stick from Emery. "What is *this*?"

"You heard the movie say a werewolf can only be killed by a silver bullet, a silver dagger, or a silver-headed walking stick. We don't have any bullets or daggers so I made us these walking sticks."

"We're going to beat off a werewolf with Mrs. M's yard-sticks and some aluminum foil?" Philip said doubtfully.

"I'm taking mine. Leave yours here if you want." Emery pointed to a note he left on the table for Mrs. Moriarty if she woke up, saying they'd gone for Philip's math book.

Philip examined the stick. *This is stupid*, he thought. *Oh well, it's better than nothing.* He followed Emery, closed the door quietly behind him, and hid the math book behind a chair on the back porch.

"Stay out of the new snow," Emery whispered. "We don't want anyone to know where we went."

Emery amazed Philip with how bossy he acted and how bravely he faced this adventure. Together they stepped into the places where something had already messed up the snow so much it wouldn't show their footprints and made their way to the house around the corner.

"We better stay in the backyards," Emery suggested.

They went across the back of one house then another and another and finally hid themselves in bushes next door to the Moster/Talbot house.

"Think anybody saw us?" Philip whispered.

"I don't think so. We're pretty small, and we stayed in the dark all the way. Even if we left a footprint or two, no one will know who the prints belong to."

The two boys studied the house in front of them. They could see the left side of it from where they hid. Emery grabbed Philip's wrist and pointed to the lighted upstairs window. A familiar shadow fluttered repeatedly across the drawn shade.

"The bat again!" Philip cried.

"Maybe it's trying to get out."

"Suppose it *gets* out and comes down where we are," Philip said fearfully, finding it harder and harder to breathe. "Aluminum foil yardsticks don't keep Dracula away."

"Oh, look. It's still trying to get out. If he comes down here we'll *have* to use the yardsticks," said Emery, keeping his eyes on the upper window. "We don't have anything else."

"What good are the yardsticks?" Philip whispered angrily. "What will we do? Measure him to death?"

"I know! A cross. We can make a cross with them. Dracula won't go near a cross."

Before Philip could answer, the light blinked out, and darkness swallowed up the shadow of the bat.

"Is it out? Is it coming?"

"Where is it? I don't see it." Both boys spun their heads frantically.

Philip finally announced. "There's nothing."

"Let's go around back," Emery suggested. "I don't like it here."

Philip followed, but bumped into Emery, who stopped abruptly. Emery pointed. In the bright moonlight they saw a line of footprints across the otherwise undisturbed snow on the wide back lawn.

"Are they... ?" Philip started.

Emery nodded. "The footprints of a giant... dog, and there aren't any people footprints next to them."

"Maybe *not* a giant dog, Emery," Philip said with a slow realization.

Emery understood. "You think they're werewolf tracks?" he asked in a helpless voice. He leaned forward to get a better look at the prints. "Awfully small feet for a werewolf."

"Look there," cried Philip, pointing.

"The box! The baby Frankenstein box!" Sitting on the back porch, its lid crookedly lying across the top, was the box they'd seen delivered to the house. At the same moment, a howl came from somewhere behind them.

"Mrs. Wenner's dog?" said Emery. "Philip, Mrs. Wenner's dog, right? You look. Tell me it's Mrs. Wenner's dog."

"I don't think so."

"Did you look?"

"No, you look."

"No, you look."

"It *has* to be Mrs. Wenner's dog."

"It *doesn't* have to be Mrs. Wenner's dog."

"We better go back to Mrs. M's," Philip said shakily.

The howl sounded again, this time closer.

"He's coming. He's coming," Emery cried and grabbed Philip's arm.

"We have to hide. Quick. Where?" Philip looked around for a safe haven.

"Oh, I don't want to be werewolf food," Emery cried, leaping up and running toward the Talbot house.

Philip followed Emery, agreeing that with a werewolf right behind them, the only safe direction was toward the house. As soon as they got near the back porch, though, the kitchen light came on and covered them with its glare.

"It'll see us," cried Emery.

"Now what!"

"In the box. Let's get in the box. It's the only place we can hide," said Emery. He didn't wait for Philip, but leaped up the steps to the porch and threw himself inside the baby Frankenstein box.

Philip threw himself on top of Emery. "Move over," he cried. "You're hogging the whole thing."

"I am not."

The boys wiggled into the best positions they could manage.

"The top," said Philip. Emery reached up and slid the top of the box into position.

"Ow! Watch your stupid knee," Philip cried softly. "That hurt!"

Suddenly, they heard the kitchen door open and a horrible snarling noise exploded right above them. They grabbed each other and held on. A howl sounded, but from much farther away than before.

Suddenly, the box moved, and they heard a door close. They'd been rolled inside the Talbot house, the home of Dracula, the Wolfman, and baby Frankenstein!

CHAPTER SEVEN

The two boys, crushed together in their heavy coats in the cramped box, scarcely drew a breath. They heard a snuffling sound outside the box; then a whistle; then a weird click-clack across the kitchen floor; then silence.

"I think it followed us inside the house," whispered Philip.

"Move your foot," Emery demanded.

"I can't. You're lying on it. Did you hear me? The werewolf's in the house."

"I know. I smelled it right outside the box. It smelled like a dog." Emery paused. "I can't smell it now; or even hear it. Can you see through a hole?"

Philip twisted his neck, but could only glance through an air hole at an angle.

"I see a chair. A kitchen chair."

"That's a lot of help," said Emery. "Do you see anybody? Any... thing?"

"Nobody's sitting in the chair. Can't you see out of a hole?"

Emery twisted his body. "Ooofff," Philip grunted. "You're mooshing my face with your elbow."

"So move your face. I can almost see..."

"Ooofff," grunted Philip again as Emery's elbow pushed hard against his nose.

"Get your stupid elbow..." whispered Philip.

"I can see pretty good now," Emery interrupted. "Nothing's in sight. Come on. We can't stay here."

"What are you... ?" Before Philip could finish his question, Emery lifted the top from the box. The boys untangled themselves from each other and slowly lifted their eyes above the sides of the box. They saw an empty kitchen, but they heard sounds coming from somewhere higher up in the house.

"Don't make any noise," Philip whispered, throwing his leg over the side and dropping to the kitchen floor.

"It must have gone upstairs," Emery responded softly, setting himself down next to Philip. After he replaced the top, Emery stuttered, "Come... come..."

"What's the matter?"

"I have to... to..."

"Not sneeze! Emery, don't. You'll sneeze us into were-wolf snacks! Hold it. Don't let it out." Philip looked the kitchen over and saw a towel hanging on the handle of the refrigerator door. He grabbed it and tossed it to Emery. Emery, his eyes wide and his cheeks puffed up in his battle with the sneeze, balled the towel up, pushed it hard against his face, and sneezed into it. Philip heard a tiny *boop*—a *boop* he hoped didn't reach the werewolf's ears.

"Make sure you're sneezed out," Philip warned.

Emery wriggled his nose trying to find another sneeze. He shook his head. "Only one." He threw the towel back to Philip, who caught it with two fingers and a look of disgust and replaced it on the refrigerator door.

"See any werewolf stuff?" Emery asked as they tiptoed to the back door.

"Like what? People's bones? Let's get out of here."

"Look, a letter addressed to Mr. Lawrence Talbot. It might be evidence. I'm taking it." He grabbed the envelope off the kitchen counter and stuffed it into his back pocket. A growl and a roar came from upstairs.

That was all the boys needed. Philip opened the back door, jumped down the steps to the lawn, found his silver-headed walking stick, and ran across the neighborhood backyards. When he squashed himself against the wall of Mrs. Moriarty's house, Emery stood next to him panting.

"Did you remember to close the door?"

Emery nodded, catching his breath. Between huffing and puffing Emery said, "I can't believe we were in the werewolf's house with it right upstairs."

"Where's your walking stick?"

"My... oh, I left it. I didn't even think about it."

"Didn't you see me pick up mine?"

"No. I just ran."

"I don't guess you want to go back for it?"

Emery's eyes grew big and round. He shook his head quickly. "It doesn't have anybody's name on it or anything."

"Mrs. Moriarty will wonder where her other yardstick went."

"Maybe we can get it tomorrow. Take your math book and let's go back in. How long have we been away?"

Philip couldn't tell so he didn't answer. He retrieved his book from behind the porch chair, and together he and Emery entered Mrs. Moriarty's kitchen. They tiptoed across the floor and checked the living room. Mrs. Moriarty still lay asleep in her chair in front of the TV. Relieved they didn't have to face any questions from Mrs. Moriarty, the boys went back into the den.

"Let's see what the letter says." Emery reached behind him and yanked out the already opened envelope. He unfolded the letter.

"What's it say? What's it say?" Philip stared over Emery's shoulder.

"It says welcome to the city of Brunton and congratulations on being selected from dozens of applicants. Please report to your new job at eight a. m. Monday, December 8, to..."

"To? To? Go ahead. To where?"

Emery looked inside the envelope for a second page. "There's no more."

"No more! The Wolfman's getting a job right here in Brunton and starts this Monday, and we don't know where? Look inside the envelope again."

Emery turned the envelope upside down and shook it.

"Did you drop the second page?"

"I only saw one page in the envelope."

The boys drifted off into deep thought. Finally, Emery said, "Maybe we should watch the rest of the movie?"

Philip gave Emery a hesitant look. "I don't think so."

"How about just the end—to see if the Wolfman is captured or what?"

"Okay, yeah okay, but I don't want to hear any of the talking in the movie. Let's go to the end and fast search backwards. We'll be able to tell what happens to him."

Emery agreed and performed the necessary button pushing. "Ready?"

Philip nodded and both boys got back on the sofa and sat close together. Emery pushed reverse. The boys watched the static on the TV screen disappear and the names of the actors roll backwards. Then they saw Larry Talbot lying on the ground. As they watched he turned back into werewolf! Another man watched the change, too.

"Isn't that his father?" Philip whispered.

"Yeah. Look, they're fighting."

"Stop it. Push the stop button."

Emery pushed the button and the screen turned blue.

"His father killed him," Philip said softly.

"You think our Larry Talbot has a father? Maybe we could call him."

"Call him and what?"

"Tell him to come over and bop his son before he starts eating people in the neighborhood," said Emery.

Philip shook his head in disdain. "I don't think so."

"But at least in the movie he died. So they can die, right?"

"I guess."

"Still watching TV?" Mrs. Moriarty stood in the door-way.

"Argh!" The boys jumped at Mrs. Moriarty's unexpected interruption.

"I guess I dozed off a few minutes. You must have had a very boring night. I haven't been much of a baby-sitter for you. Are you hungry?"

Both boys shook their heads.

"Okay. Your family just drove into the driveway, Emery. Might as well get ready to go home. They'll call any moment." Mrs. Moriarty cocked her head and looked oddly at the two boys. "You both sure you're okay?"

Both boys nodded energetically.

Mrs. Moriarty smiled and left the room.

"Put the yardstick back," said Emery.

Philip had carried the yardstick into the den with him. He picked up the yardstick, pulled the aluminum foil off the top, and froze. "Emery. Emery. Come see."

Emery walked over to him. "What?"

"Look."

Emery inspected the yardstick and *he* froze. Deep bite marks of something very large covered the yardstick.

CHAPTER EIGHT

"Don't forget, Philip, we're having dinner over the Wyatt's tonight."

"Why are you shouting?" asked Philip, who stood right behind his mother.

His mother jumped. "Philip, I thought you were in the living room."

"No, kitchen. I'm hungry."

"I'll make you a sandwich."

"Do we have cracked pepper turkey? With mayonnaise and lettuce?"

"When did you get so sandwich fussy?" His father asked this question. He'd just entered the kitchen from the basement. He rubbed his hand across the top of Philip's head a few times and smiled. "A fancy sandwich may be all we'll get for dinner tonight."

"No, we won't," said Mrs. Felton. "I happen to know Emery's mother has already bought a ham and plans to drive the two babies to her sister's house so she can concentrate on cooking and entertaining tonight. Philip, all I can find is ham for your sandwich."

"Ham! How many times am I supposed to eat ham in one day?"

"This ham sandwich will be just as good as the other hundreds of ham sandwiches I've fixed for you. With mustard. The brown kind. And cut off the crust."

"If it was cracked pepper turkey, I'd eat the crust," Philip grumbled.

"I'll get some on my next trip to the store."

"Don't forget to buy mayonnaise."

"And lettuce. I heard you the first time, darling."

Philip sat at the table and watched his mother put his sandwich together.

"Who are the other people coming to dinner tonight?" his father asked.

"Some friends of Betty's. They just moved into the neighborhood. I think they knew each other in high school."

Philip's stomach exploded. "The people from the haunted house?" he blurted.

"You mean the one you and Emery fixed up?" said his father.

Philip nodded.

"I don't know. Are they the new neighbors?"

"I don't know. I guess. Betty said they just moved into the neighborhood. The Talbots."

"I gotta go," said Philip.

"Sit, sit, sit, mister. I didn't make this sandwich for nothing."

Philip sat back down and decided the quickest way out of the kitchen was to eat the sandwich and run. Emery had to know about this—if he didn't know already.

Ten minutes later, Philip banged on the Wyatt's front door. Emery's mom answered.

"Oh, hello, Philip." Mrs. Wyatt held a baby in her arms, and Philip could hear the other baby crying in the background.

"Is Emery home?"

"He's in his room, and he won't come out."

"Why not?"

"Come in. I fed one, but not the other," she said wearily, as if this was something Philip needed to know.

Philip followed Mrs. Wyatt into the living room and watched her put one baby down and pick up the other baby. He knew the two babies were only about one year apart. The baby she put down started wobbling around the living room on very shaky legs. Mrs. Wyatt took a bottle of milk and stuffed the nipple into the crying baby's mouth.

"No, no, no," she said to the wobbly baby, who grabbed onto a lamp cord for balance. Mrs. Wyatt switched the smaller baby to her other arm and grabbed the arm of the wobbly baby.

This is going to take forever, Philip thought. "Can I go up to see Emery?"

"No, you can't have this bottle. You just had yours. No, no, now stop it."

Philip tried again. "Can I go up to see Emery?"

"Don't pull your diaper off. Now stop it."

"Can I go up to see Emery?"

"He's in his room, and he won't come out."

"I know. You already told me."

"Why won't he come out?"

"How should I know?" Philip said, perplexed.

"OW! Don't pinch me," Emery's mother snapped. She released the walking baby, who wobbled right back to the dangling electrical cord. "No, no. I said no."

Philip began to understand about the headaches Emery said his mother got. He'd try another approach. "I'm going up to see Emery. Okay?"

"What is so fascinating about a lamp cord? Yes, go, Philip. Go. He's in his room, and he won't come out."

Philip went up the stairs as fast as politeness would allow, all the while listening to Mrs. Wyatt in the background discussing the electrical cord with a one-year-old who wanted the cord more than she had ever wanted anything in her life.

Philip knocked on Emery's closed door.

"No," came Emery's voice in a shout. "No, I'm not coming out. I'm staying right here, and I'm not coming out until tomorrow, and you can't make me. No, no, no."

Philip opened the door slightly. "Emery?"

"No, I said I'm... Philip? What are you doing here?"

"I was having lunch when my mom said we're eating here tonight with..."

"I know. I know. Lawrence Talbot is coming here. With his family. They'll *all* be here; him, Dracula, and baby Frankenstein."

"Isn't his family a wife and a little girl?"

"Who knows? Maybe they're his family during the day before the moon comes up, but what about after? Who are they then? I'm not leaving my room. N-O!"

"Maybe it'll be all right if our moms and dads are there."

"What difference will *that* make? Are moms and dads stronger than the power of the full moon? Can moms and dads keep you from having your blood sucked right out of you? Larry Talbot is coming here for a reason, and I'm the reason."

"What do you mean you're the reason? Why's your hand under the pillow?"

Emery withdrew the hidden hand and thrust it at Philip as if he were a prince and expected Philip to kiss it. After two seconds of confusion, Philip saw what Emery wanted him to see. There on the back of Emery's left hand was a five-pointed star. *A pentagram!*

"I'm going to be the werewolf's next victim," said Emery.

CHAPTER NINE

"What's that? Where did you get it?" Philip asked in alarm.

"The library. I went to the library this morning, and they had a little fair on the top floor to raise money. You showed your library card, and they stamped your hand so you could go upstairs. This is the stamp."

Philip thought a moment. "But then everybody at the library got a stamp like you."

"Yeah, but *they* don't live down the street from... you-know-what. *They* don't know the truth about this neighborhood. *They* don't know what we know. And *he's* not having dinner at *their* house tonight." Emery lowered his head into his right palm, a picture of surrender.

"It's just an accident you got the mark. The one in the movie was like... magical. It appeared and then it disappeared. Nobody stamped it there, and only Bela the Wolfman could see it."

"It doesn't mean it really happens that way. Maybe it happens this way. Maybe somebody puts it on you. You want a pentagram? Here." Emery grabbed a red magic marker and yanked the top off. "I'll give you one. Give me your hand."

"No, no. Forget it." Philip zipped both hands behind his back.

"Come on. Come on. It won't be a magical pentagram, so it won't make any difference you said." Emery jumped on Philip and knocked him down. They wrestled around as Emery tried to draw on the back of Philip's hand, and Philip tried to stop him.

"What's all the noise up there?" Emery's mother shouted up the stairs. "I'm trying to put the babies down for naps. Whatever you two are doing, stop it!"

The boys sat on the floor breathing hard. Philip gave Emery an angry look. "Some friend you are—trying to give me a werewolf pentagram."

"So? You said it didn't matter. Remember?"

"All right. All right. It *might* matter. We don't know yet."

"Yet? Good, let's wait until tonight and find out. You can tell me while the Wolfman's chewing on my shoulder. What are we going to do about it?"

Philip almost answered, *What do you mean, we?* but thought better of it.

"You're positive he's coming here tonight?"

"*Yes,* he's coming here tonight. What a stupid question. And he's coming for *me.*" Emery waved the back of his hand in Philip's face.

"I see it. I see it. Well, the answer's simple. Don't be here when he comes."

"Where am I going to go? You gonna buy me a bus ticket to New Jersey? I can't just leave the house."

Philip got up off the floor. "I'm going home. Let me think about it."

"How will I know if you get an idea? I'm *not* leaving this room. Help me move the bed against the door. The bureau, too."

"How will I get out then? You can move stuff later. There's no hurry 'cause he can't change until after dark, right? You don't have to hide until then. Come to my house in a little while. I'll have a plan by then."

"Well, okay, but I'm going to be back in here with my bureau against the door way before it gets dark."

Philip walked thoughtfully down the street toward his house. When he reached home, his father sat on the sofa, his baby sister Becky asleep next to him. His father waved him over.

"What's this?" his father asked with a smile.

"Oh, my spelling test."

"100%. Very good."

Philip shrugged, his mind elsewhere.

"Close your eyes and put out your hand."

Philip followed his father's directions. First, he felt his father's finger press onto the back of his hand. Then his father flipped his hand over and put something into it. Philip opened his eyes and saw a dollar bill.

"Just a small reward for your fine test."

"Thanks, Dad. But why did you... ?" Philip turned his hand over to see why his father pressed his finger there.

A feeling of shock and horror swept over Philip. Shining brightly on the back of his hand was a tiny, shiny gold star, the kind they gave out in first grade. *A golden pentagram!*

"What's this? Where'd you get it?"

"Oh, I found a box of them downstairs in the basement and thought I'd surprise you with one. I can see you're surprised."

"Yeah. Surprised. Can I take it off?"

Philip's father shrugged. "Do what you want." Becky stirred and Mr. Felton picked her up and walked with her into the kitchen. "Time for a feeding, sweetheart," he said to his wife.

Impossible, thought Philip. Impossible, but true. Both he and Emery had been marked with the sign of the pentagram! Not like the movie one that appeared then disappeared, but a *real* pentagram. How could this have happened? How?

Philip ran upstairs, slammed his bedroom door, and wondered how long it would take him to slide his bed and bureau against the door. He and Emery were under attack!

CHAPTER TEN

"I can't believe our mothers threw us out of the house," Philip moaned.

Emery agreed. "Yeah, usually we get yelled at 'cause we *don't* want to go to our rooms, and today we get thrown out because we *do* want to go to our rooms. It's not fair. Now we have to have dinner tonight with you-know-who, and both of us marked with the sign of the pentagram. Oh, this is bad. This is really, really bad."

The two boys walked around the block tucked into their heavy coats and wearing wool caps pulled down over their ears. Emery had scrubbed the inky star off the back of his hand with his toothbrush and soap, and was *not* looking forward to brushing his teeth that night. After Philip showed his golden pentagram to Emery he peeled it off and tossed it away. Even though the pentagrams were gone, the boys couldn't mistake their meaning.

"I knew I should have moved the bed and bureau over to the door," Emery went on. "But I couldn't move either one. They were both too heavy, so I stuck some socks under the door."

"Socks? Why? You think the smell would keep monsters away?"

"My socks don't smell. Anyway, they were clean socks from my drawer."

"Whatever. What did you do it for?"

"I jammed them under the door and hoped the door would get stuck and not open."

"Did it work?" If it did, Philip thought he could use the trick.

"I'm here. Don't you see me?"

"Didn't work, eh?"

Emery didn't bother to answer. After a few more steps he said, "We need a plan. You said you'd have plan by now."

"I didn't know I'd need a plan for both of us."

"So you got one or not? You don't, do you?"

"How about if we both get sick and have to stay in bed?"

"Like our moms'll really believe us after we locked ourselves in our rooms."

"Did your mother ask you if you were crazy? Mine did."

"Your mom asked you if I was crazy?"

"No, no. She asked me if *I* was crazy, but she said I was acting as crazy as you."

"As crazy as me! Who told her I was crazy?"

"Your mom called," Philip said wearily, "and said you wouldn't come out of your room. So my mom came to ask me if I knew what was wrong with you, but I was locked in my room and wouldn't come out. That's when she asked me if I was crazy and said something about being at a strange age."

"Her? How old is she?"

"Not her; us, dummy. Then she threw me out."

"Oh, we need a plan," Emery wailed in desperation. "We need a plan bad."

"I'm thinking. I'm thinking. Just be quiet."

"Be quiet. Be quiet. Everybody tells me to be quiet. I have to be quiet at home because of babies. I have to be quiet in school because of the teacher. I have to be quiet in the supermarket so my mother can concentrate on shopping. I have to be quiet now so you can think. I should have been born without mouth. When I grow up I'm going to be the noisiest grown-up ever. I'm going to…"

"Supermarket, Emery! Do you have any money?"

"On me? No."

"How about at home?"

"Some. I think four dollars. Why?"

"I have some, too. Let's get our money and go to the supermarket."

"Why?"

"When I tell you my plan, you'll see why."

As the boys hurried back home to get their money, Philip explained his plan.

"What time are they supposed to get here?" Philip whispered to Emery as they huddled together that evening on the sofa in Emery's living room.

"Seven-thirty. Same as your family. What do you think his wife looks like? If he's the werewolf, she must be the Dracula. I wonder if she'll wear her cape. A lady Dracula and a baby Frankenstein daughter," Emery moaned. "The daughter's probably got lines all over her."

"Lines?"

"You know. You saw the movie. The monster had lines where they sewed him together. The little girl probably has them, too. Maybe we can pull her apart at the seams."

"Emery, we're not going to pull her apart and have blood and skin and stuff flying all over your living room. Did you check to see if the supermarket stuff is where we hid it?"

"I did. It's all there. It's..."

DING-DONG

Philip and Emery looked at each other. Dracula, Wolfman, and baby Frankenstein had arrived!

CHAPTER ELEVEN

Emery's mother passed by on her way to answer the doorbell. The two boys heard the door open, some grown-up chatter, and then Lawrence Talbot appeared. After he handed his coat to Emery's father, he turned and saw the boys huddled on the sofa and smiled at them.

Philip and Emery didn't return the smile. They could only stare at the tall, fuzzy-bearded man dressed in black slacks and a white shirt looking back at them. Emery's father said, "This is Mr. Talbot, boys. This is my son Emery and his friend Philip. Honey, take Larry into the den."

Mr. Talbot spoke to the boys in a deep voice. "I'll want to meet you later—in private." Emery's mother accompanied Mr. Talbot to the den, leaving the boys staring at their backs, eyes wide, mouths open.

"Did he say he wanted to *eat* us later in private?" Emery whispered in a panic.

"I don't know," Philip replied anxiously. "I couldn't pay attention. I think he said he wanted to *meet* us, but it could have been *eat* us."

"Yeah. Meet us to eat us," said Emery.

A woman stepped into the living room. Emery's dad took her coat and introduced the two boys. "This is Ms. Moster, boys, Mr. Talbot's wife. The boys seem to be a little shy tonight. This is my son Emery and his friend Philip."

The woman, tall and thin like her husband, wore a black dress and bright red lipstick. She smiled at the boys and said, "It's going to be such a nice night." She turned to attend to her daughter.

"Nice bite! Did she say nice bite?" whispered a panicky Emery.

"I thought she said bite. But maybe she said night. I don't know. She could have said fight, sight, right, or schmight. I can't pay attention."

"Did you see her bloody mouth? Maybe she ate already and won't want to suck us dry."

"That was lipstick, wasn't it?"

"Was it? Oh," moaned Emery. "Here comes baby Frankenstein."

A little girl no more than three years old handed her coat to her mother, who handed it to Emery's father. The little girl began jumping up and down. "Go play with the boys," said Emery's father, and he escorted Ms. Moster down the hallway to the den.

The little girl stopped jumping and studied the boys. She clutched a small bag to her side. She took two more jumps, and each time she jumped, Philip and Emery's hearts jumped, too. The girl stood still and studied them some more.

"Stay right there," said Emery. "Don't come any closer. What's your name?"

"One, two, fwee." She made one last big jump and got near enough to touch the boys, who sat in frozen horror a mere foot away from her.

"*You got lines?*" Emery cried, pulling his legs up under him.

"Put out your hand," Philip ordered.

"You see any lines?" Emery whispered.

"Not yet. Ask her her name again."

"What's your name, little girl?"

She jumped up and said, "One, two, fwee. Me Fwankie. Fwankie, Fwankie, Fwankie."

"Fwankie? I mean Frankie?" said Emery. "It's really Frankie? You got lines? You do, don't you. Are you all sewn together?"

The little girl bent over and reached into her bag. Emery and Philip gasped.

"One, two, fwee. I got birdie." She pulled a metal bird from the bag and shot her arm stiffly up into the air.

Emery and Philip reared back and let out short screams.

"What is it?" Emery gasped.

"Birdie, birdie, birdie," the girl answered.

"It's a birdie, birdie, birdie," said Philip.

"Birdie fwy. See birdie fwy." The little girl shook the toy bird up and down and seemed thrilled to death to watch the wings flap up and down. She ran around the room shaking

96

the bird wildly until the wings fluttered up and down so fast they were hard to follow.

Emery's father appeared and said, "Come on, Frankie, Philip, Emery. We're going to eat. Take her into the dining room, Emery."

"Wait, Dad. We'll go with you." Emery leaped from the sofa, and Philip leaped with him.

"Fwy your birdie, birdie, birdie this way," said Philip, and little Frankie followed the boys into the dining room.

Soon, the three families sat around the table. Philip and Emery took seats next to one another diagonally across from Lawrence Talbot. Ms. Moster sat across from her husband, next to Emery. Frankie sat in a highchair by her mother's side.

"Ask if her name's really Frankie," Philip whispered to Emery as everyone watched Frankie wriggling and giggling in her seat.

Emery leaned forward toward his father, who sat across from him. "Is the little girl really named Frankie?"

Ms. Moster heard him and turned to Emery. "We named her Frances, but somehow we ended up calling her Frankie."

"She got lines?" Emery asked, and Philip whacked Emery in the ribs with his elbow.

"Lines?" Ms. Moster's forehead wrinkled.

"Nothing, nothing," said Philip.

Frankie started screaming, "Eat boys. Eat boys." She started laughing too hard to say any more.

Philip and Emery turned slowly to one another. Emery nodded. Philip rose and walked to the china closet. He pulled open the door and reached way back behind the blue dishes his mother never used. He took out two cardboard shakers and brought them back to the table.

"She's always so noisy at dinnertime," Ms. Moster explained. "We tell her when she eats not to make any noise. She's saying eat and noise."

"She said, 'Eat boys,'" Emery argued, unconvinced. "Philip and I are the only boys here."

"I don't think she wants to eat the two of you," Ms. Moster said with a chuckle.

"Ha, ha," Emery said coldly.

"She can't say the word noise yet," Ms Moster explained.

"Eat boys. Ha, ha, ha."

"Frankie, no noise," Lawrence Talbot said severely, and Frankie quieted.

"She's scared of him," Emery whispered to Philip.

"So am I," Philip whispered back.

"Philip, what have you got there?" Philip's mom had discovered the shakers.

"Uh, stuff we like for our food," said Philip.

Mr. Felton reached for Philip's shaker. He sniffed at it. "Uhh. Garlic? Is this garlic?"

Philip and Emery had bought two shakers of garlic powder on their visit to the supermarket earlier. They knew from the movies that garlic protected people from vampires. They had taken off the paper wrapper identifying it as garlic, hoping no one would notice.

"Uh, yeah, Dad. Garlic. The teacher said garlic was... was good for you. Said we should eat it at every meal. We love it, don't we, Emery?"

Emery nodded rapidly and smacked his lips. "Oh, yeah. Love that garlic."

"Your teacher said garlic was good for you?" Mr. Talbot repeated doubtfully.

Philip let Emery deal with Mr. Talbot while he reached across the table to take a roll from a basket of rolls. He broke the roll in half and shook his garlic shaker over the two pieces of roll. He handed one piece to Emery.

"Not so much..." Emery's mother began.

Emery and Philip bit into their rolls. Immediately, their mouths filled with a taste so sour they could hardly stand it. The taste made both boys take deep breaths through their noses, and a lot of the loose powder went up their noses along with the air.

"*AAHH CHOOO!*" Philip exploded, the bread in his mouth sailing across the table and landing on Lawrence Talbot's plate. "*AAHH CHOOO!*"

"*AAHH CHOOO!*" Emery echoed, the bread in his mouth sailing across the table and plopping into Lawrence Talbot's water glass.

"*AAHH CHOOO! AAHH CHOOO! AAHH CHOOO! AAHH CHOOO!*" the two boys chorused.

Emery's mother and Philip's mother jumped up and rushed to their sons, napkins in hand. Philip and Emery took the napkins, finished their sneezing, and wiped the sneezing tears from their eyes.

"Maybe we'll just save this for later," said Mr. Felton, putting the boys' two shakers of garlic out of reach.

Emery's mom picked up the two crumpled napkins Mr. Talbot had folded in front of him, one holding Philip's bread, the other holding Emery's soggy bread.

"I'm so sorry," she apologized, her face turning pink. She hurried into the kitchen to throw the napkins away and get Mr. Talbot a new glass of water. When she returned, she held two Popsicle sticks bound together with a rubber band to make a cross.

"I'll take that, Mom," said Emery.

"What is it? I took four of these out of the refrigerator earlier."

Philip and Emery had also bought a big box of craft sticks at the supermarket and had spent much of the afternoon making crosses and hiding them in strategic places around the house.

Emery put the cross down in front of him. Philip slowly reached over and slid the cross next to his plate.

"Hey," said Emery.

"It's one I made," Philip whispered insistently.

"What is it for?" asked Philip's father.

"School," Philip answered nervously. "We need it for school."

"School?" Lawrence Talbot said in a puzzled voice. "What kind of a school makes you eat garlic and need Popsicle stick crosses?"

"Well, it's... it's like... well, tell him, Emery."

"Well, like Philip said, it's... it's like... well..."

"Yeah," said Philip, seeing Emery going nowhere. "Just stuff we do. You know."

"Hmmm, what kind of a school... ?" muttered Lawrence Talbot again before his voice trailed off.

"Have some salad," said Mrs. Wyatt, placing a large bowl of greens onto the dining table along with a big pair of plastic spoons attached like scissors to serve the salad.

Philip's father looked at Philip and smiled. "Would you like some garlic on yours? How about you, Emery?"

"Oh, well no, Dad."

"No, thanks," said Emery.

"Garlic, anyone?"

A tiny laugh went around the table. Philip noticed, though, the laugh stopped at Lawrence Talbot who merely sat in deep thought.

Suddenly, little Frankie started shouting, "Stick, stick, stick. See big stick."

She pointed as she shouted.

"No, noise," said Lawrence Talbot.

Emery's mother looked toward the corner where Frankie pointed and saw two yardsticks tucked against the wall.

"What in the world? Who put them there?" Mrs. Wyatt mumbled. She walked over and lifted up the two yardsticks, the bottom end of each covered with bulging layers of aluminum foil held on with rubber bands. She brought them back to the table. "Emery? Now what?" The boys had gotten yardsticks and aluminum paper at the supermarket also.

"School, again?" Lawrence Talbot asked with growing surprise. Philip couldn't understand the look on the man's face. Frightened, angry, puzzled, entertained? It was a weird, weird look, though, on a weird, weird face. That's all Philip knew.

"Well, yeah. Philip and I... we... we're. Tell them, Philip."

"Well, it's for a show."

"Yeah, it's for a show." Emery nodded in agreement.

"And what kind of a show would that be?" Lawrence Talbot asked, smiling, it seemed to Philip, most devilishly.

The look on Lawrence Talbot's face drove all thoughts out of Philip's mind. He could only stare and wonder what this man would do next. It was already dark outside, and he could probably change anytime he wanted to if he didn't mind doing it front of all these people. Philip wondered whether werewolves were shy. He bet they probably weren't.

Emery came to the rescue. "It's a... a dancing show."

"Dancing?" Philip tried hard to not make it sound like a question.

"Yeah, right, remember. Come on." Emery rose and took the two sticks from his mother. He handed one to Philip. "Get up. We'll show them. *Get up!*"

What is Emery talking about? Philip asked himself. *Show them what?* He stood up, though, and watched Emery.

Emery started banging the wooden end of his yardstick on the rug, holding tightly to the aluminum at the top. As he banged the yardstick up and down, he hopped quickly in a circle around it, alternately landing flat on his left foot, then on the toes of his right foot.

"Come on," said Emery, and Philip could see the panic rising in his friend's eyes.

Philip started banging his yardstick and hopping around in a circle, his right foot landing on the toe, his left hitting flat.

"It's a singing and a dancing show," Emery called over the noise of the stick. "We didn't learn the song yet, but it's a good dance. Watch."

As he danced and hopped, he moved across the dining room toward the stairway to the second floor. Philip followed him, hopping and dancing crazily. Philip felt like an idiot and thought Emery looked like a moron. He didn't look at his parents because he knew what they must be thinking. Like Emery, though, he wanted to get away from the table and away from Lawrence Talbot.

"What in the world is going on in their school? I found a yardstick just like those outside my house," Philip heard Lawrence Talbot say as he and Emery danced out of the room to the bottom of the stairs. Philip heard Lawrence Talbot's voice again. "Can I go talk to them?"

"Be my guest, if you don't think it will spoil your appetite," Emery's father responded.

"He's coming," Philip cried, and he and Emery charged up the stairs. "Where'll we hide?"

"The babies' room. The babies' room." They ducked into the middle bedroom, and the boys dove behind one of the two baby cribs. They heard footsteps coming up the stairs. Outside their bedroom door they heard Lawrence Talbot's voice, "Philip. Emery. Where are you?"

Emery's mouth moved quickly, but Philip couldn't make out in the dim light what he said. Finally, he heard Emery cry, "One, two, three." Emery burst out from behind his crib and ran to the door. Philip could think of nothing else to do but follow him. They leaped out into the hallway.

"Oh, there you are."

"Ahhhh!" Emery turned and tossed his yardstick at Lawrence Talbot.

"Hey!"

Philip ran straight ahead and stuck the aluminum foil end into Lawrence Talbot's stomach like a sword.

"Ouch! What... ?"

"The basement," Emery screamed and down the stairs the boys bounded.

Philip followed Emery around the corner from the dining room and down into the dark cellar. Emery grabbed Philip and pulled him into a tiny closet his father had built to store cans of food and rolls of paper goods. They stood quietly in the dark and caught their breath.

"Maybe the silver-headed walking sticks finished him," Emery whispered.

"How could they? They weren't silver. They're only aluminum foil."

"Aluminum foil's silver. It's silver enough. It better be."

"We left our crosses at the table," Philip said between breaths.

"Maybe we can breathe garlic breath on him."

"If he's close enough for us to breathe garlic on, we're dead ducks."

The lights flashed on. Both boys sucked in great breaths and held onto them. Footsteps descended the stairs. When the footsteps stopped, Emery whispered in as small a voice as he could manage.

"When I say three, up and through the dining room and out the kitchen door. One, two three."

Emery threw the door open and ran up the cellar stairs, charging past his father, Philip right behind him. Emery slipped going around the corner from the basement to the dining room, and Philip tumbled on top of him. They scrambled to their feet quickly, Philip now in front, and tore straight into the dining room toward the kitchen.

"Ahhh! He's here," Philip cried, seeing Mr. Talbot back in his dining chair and screeching to a stop. "Turn around! Turn around."

"We're trapped," Emery shrieked.

"Turn around!" Philip pushed his way past Emery as Mrs. Wyatt approached the table holding a tray full of bowls with steam rising from them.

Emery grabbed Philip and tried to get in front again. Philip pushed him away and together they smashed into

Mrs. Wyatt, who stood still as a statue, amazed at the spectacle of the two horrified boys. The tray went one way, and the bowls went the other. The tray clanked against the table before coming to rest on the floor. The bowls crashed down on the table right in front of Lawrence Talbot. They bounced and hit him in the chest and arms, and one rolled gently into his lap.

"Yow!" Mr. Talbot cried and jumped up.

"Philip!" shrieked Mrs. Felton. "Look what you've done! You just covered the new assistant principal of your school with hot chicken noodle soup!"

CHAPTER TWELVE

There was no dinner that night. After much apologizing but little explaining, the families agreed to have dinner the next night. In a restaurant. They agreed to leave all the children at home with baby sitters.

The following evening, Emery's aunt came over to mind the two babies. Philip's aunt came to mind baby Becky. A Talbot cousin came to take care of little Frankie, and Emery and Philip ended up at Mrs. Moriarty's.

"I hear you boys had an interesting evening last night," Mrs. Moriarty said when the two boys arrived and slumped mournfully onto her sofa.

"My father called me a nincompoop," Emery reported in a sad voice.

Mrs. Moriarty laughed. "That's not good."

"My father kept asking my mother whether she brought the right baby home from the hospital," said Philip.

Mrs. Moriarty laughed again. "That's not good either."

"My mother keeps finding the crosses we made with the Popsicle sticks all over the house. Sixty-four of them so far. She told my father, and that's when he called me a nincompoop."

"Well, you two certainly got yourselves a strange notion about your new assistant principal."

Philip and Emery moaned in unison at the words *new assistant principal.*

"We're gonna have to see him in school *every* day," Emery mumbled glumly.

"And we don't graduate to another school for more than two years," Philip muttered from deep in his gloom.

"If he lets us out at all," Emery added. "Maybe we'll be lucky, and he'll throw us out of school right away."

"How did your parents explain things to Mr. Talbot?"

"My dad told him I was a nincompoop and promised to punish me," said Emery.

"Did he yet?" Philip asked.

"I think he's going to cancel Christmas."

"Wow!" Mrs. Moriarty sympathized. "What about you, Philip?"

"I had to go over to Mr. Talbot's house this morning with my dad and apologize and explain."

"You didn't tell me that," said Emery.

"I didn't see you till now."

"You poor boy," Mrs. Moriarty laughed. "Well, I guess I'll go fix dinner."

When Mrs. Moriarty left, Emery said, "What did you tell Mr. Wolfman about us?"

"That we thought he was a werewolf."

Emery moaned, clutching at his forehead. "What'd he say?"

"He said if we wouldn't call him 'Mr. Wolfman' in school, he wouldn't call us the chicken noodle dancing assassins."

Emery moaned again. "Like we would. But all the clues were there. What about his name?"

"He said his father and his grandfather were both named Lawrence, and his grandfather lived way before the movie we saw. His name had nothing to do with the movie."

"What about the bat flying in the window? We both saw it."

"Little *Fwankie* has a stick for her stupid bird," Philip explained disgustedly. "That's why she knew the word *stick* at dinner. She puts the bird on the stick and makes it *fwy*. From outside through the shade... well, you know what it looks like."

"What about her baby Frankenstein box?"

"Their dog came in it. We heard their dog howling. Mrs. Wenner's dog smelled it or heard and kept howling to it, and they howled back and forth at each other. The night we were in his yard, we heard Mrs. Wenner's dog howling at their dog. Mrs. Wenner's dog must have put the teethmarks on the yardstick I brought back with us. I don't know why she lets such a dangerous dog run around loose. When we were in the box, Mr. Talbot's dog sniffed around us. It's a good thing the family called it upstairs, or we would never have gotten out."

"Does he know we were in his house?"

"I don't think so. He didn't say anything, and neither did I."

"So the job in the letter was to be our new assistant principal."

Philip nodded and Emery moaned again.

Mrs. Moriarty poked her head back into the living room. "I got you boys a movie. It's in the machine. Just push play. You can watch some of it now while I cook and finish the rest of it after dinner."

"Want to?" Philip asked in a quiet voice, his mind still focused on his dancing like a crazy string puppet in Emery's dining room in front of his new assistant principal.

Emery shrugged, reached for the remote, pushed *Play*, and the movie began.

The movie was in black and white. A thick test tube sent heavy white smoke swirling across the screen. The title of the movie melted down from the top of the TV and spelled out:

FRANKENSTEIN MEETS THE WOLFMAN

Both boys sat hypnotized as the names of the players swirled down onto the screen. Finally, their worst fears came true.

AND LON CHANEY, JR. AS THE WOLFMAN

The boys stared, frozen in fearful wonder.

On the screen, a full moon sits in the night sky while heavy clouds rush all around it. A sign appears: HERE REST THE DEAD OF LLANWELLY. Two men walk through the dark cemetery. Leaves, driven by a brisk wind, fly all around. A crow caws spookily.

"Where are they going?" Emery whispered.
"I don't know. Watch."

The two men go down some broad steps and walk through the graves until they come to a large, stone crypt. There are big letters across the top, above the door.

"TALBOT," Philip whispered, reading the letters.

The two men climb through a window above the door.

"I don't think they're supposed to go in there," said Emery.
"I know, I know," said Philip. "Shhh."

The two men look around. They read, Martin Talbot, 1837; Elizabeth Talbot, 1845. They keep looking until they come to an enormous stone casket right in the middle of the floor. One of the men reads a plaque on the outside of the lid. "Lawrence Stewart Talbot, Who Died at the Youthful Age of Thirty-one. R. I. P."

"What's R. I. P.?" Philip asked.
"It probably means Really Interesting Person," Emery replied with certainty.
Philip gave him a look. "I think *you're* an R. I. P."
"Look," said Emery. "It's the one they want. They're opening it!"
"Shh. Listen."
One man says, "This gives me the creeps. What do you think it'll look like after so many years?"
"Just bones and an empty skull. Watch the lamp."
The other man moves the lamp, and they open the casket.
"Give me the light."
Whatever is in the casket is covered with sticks and leaves. The two men start pulling the sticks and leaves away.
"Wolfbane," says one.
"Wolfbane?"
"Yeah.

> *Even a man who is pure in heart*
> *And says his prayers by night*
> *May become a wolf when the wolfbane blooms*
> *And the autumn moon is bright.*

Now the lantern light moves up the body—

"It's him," says Emery, breathlessly. "It's Lawrence Talbot."

"He's not just bones and an empty skull," said Philip.

One man says, "Let's get on with it."
"First the ring."
The men take the ring off the dead finger and stare at it.
One man says, "Gold."

"Look!" said Philip. "The dead guy's hand's moving. He
grabbed the guy!"

Horror crosses the face of one man. "It's holding me.
Help me! Help me!"
The other man's eyes open wide. "Alive!" is all he says.
"Help me! Help me!"
The free man drops the lantern onto the wolfbane on the
floor and a small fire starts. He backs away.
"Don't leave me," the captured man begs, but his friend
climbs back out the window, and the last we see of him he is
running through the cemetery.

"Turn it off!" begged Philip. "Turn it off!"

"Where's the remote?" Emery asked in panic.

"You have it."

"Where? Where? I don't have it."

"It's in your hand, you dope."

Emery pushed a button, and the movie disappeared.

When, a few moments later, Mrs. Moriarty popped her
head back into the room and said, "Dinner," she was surprised to see the TV showing Sylvester the cat climbing up
Tweety Bird's bird cage pole.

"What happened to the movie I got for you?"

"Oh... we... we saw it before," said Philip. "We took this
other one from your shelf. But thanks."

"Yeah, thanks," said Emery. "We don't need to watch
scary movies anymore since we finished our projects."

"Did you finally choose a topic, Philip?" Mrs. Moriarty
asked as the three of them settled down at the kitchen table.

"Yeah," Philip said in embarrassment. "I did yesterday.
My dad told me what to do."

"And?"

"He said if Emery could do a report on being scared, I should be able to do a report on misunderstanding."

Mrs. Moriarty laughed. "If you get stuck, I'm sure you can ask Emery for some help." Mrs. Moriarty laughed again. "Well, enjoy your spaghetti. After dinner I have some ice cream, and you can watch all the cartoons you want."

"Maybe I'll eat so much ice cream I'll get sick and have to stay home from school. Until I'm sixteen," said Philip.

Mrs. Moriarty smiled reassuringly. "Oh, you're lucky Mr. Talbot has a sense of humor. Don't worry. It'll be all right. Oh, maybe after dinner you could show me the dance you have to do for school. I heard it's very entertaining."

Emery moaned and, with deep sighs, both boys lowered their heads and concentrated on twirling their saucy spaghetti around their forks.

Philip and the Fortune Teller
DEDICATION

To Bud and Lou
And
W. W. Jacobs

CHAPTER ONE

Philip cowered in the bushes that jutted out near the old woman's garage and gently moved some twigs aside to peek out. There she stood, dressed in a long, ragged black dress, her scraggly gray hair blowing about her shoulders, holding onto her porch railing and looking out over her yard for him.

All he had done was to toss his ball against her garage door as he walked past her house. Bang went the ball and bang went the old lady, bolting out of her rocking chair, pointing at him, and cackling at him to get away; stay away; don't come back. The old woman took him by such surprise that his ball bounced off his knee and into the street and rolled down the sewer. A perfectly good ball only two weeks old, wasted.

This old lady had already phoned his house twice before with stupid complaints about him. Once, she said he stuck his tongue out at her. Ridiculous, Philip thought, as he kept his eye on her. Emery had given him a piece of the sourest candy he'd ever tasted. He'd spit it out and waggled his tongue around, trying to get the sourness to go away.

The other time the old woman told his mother he'd made a nasty gesture at her. *Ridiculous again,* Philip thought. He and Emery had walked by, and Philip saw a mangy cat sitting on the roof of the porch where the old woman rocked on a chair directly under the cat. The cat's tail seemed to wag in time with the old lady's rocking. Philip pointed to show Emery. Who wouldn't point at such a funny sight?

The old woman jumped up, cackling as always, and a moment later, she bustled inside to her telephone. Philip's father told him to use another street to get where he was going and stay off Van Kirk Street, where she lived. Philip didn't want a third phone call, so he dived into the bushes before the old woman could get a good look at him. He hoped.

A whistling noise caught his attention, and he turned and saw Emery walking down the sidewalk. Philip waited for Emery to get nearer.

"Emery! Emery!"

Emery stopped and looked around.

"Philip?"

"Yeah."

"Where are you?"

"Here."

"Here, where?"

"Here, here."

"You can't be here. I'm here. You must be there."

Philip clenched his jaw. Emery was starting up already.

"Cut it out, Emery. In the bushes."

Emery stepped closer to the bushes and saw Philip.

"What are you doing in there?"

Philip shushed him and pointed.

"Oh, her again. Let me in."

Philip shuffled over, and Emery scrouched in next to him.

"Why are you hiding?"

Philip explained.

"You sure she didn't recognize you?" Emery asked.

"I don't think she did. I pulled my hat down real fast. That's why I missed the ball, and it rolled down the sewer." Philip wore a red Phillies cap.

"Hide your cap, and let's go out that way. She won't see us."

Philip followed Emery's suggestion, and a few minutes later the two boys walked calmly down a different street. It was Wednesday morning, the fifth day of summer vacation, and both boys were in a good mood.

"Wait'll you hear," said Emery.

"Wait'll I hear what?"

"I got a wish."

"Everybody's got wishes. I wish that old lady would move to New Jersey."

"No, no. I made a wish come true."

Philip sighed. He couldn't *wait* to hear Emery explain *this*.

"Go ahead," Philip muttered. "Let's hear."

"I just came from where they're setting up the circus. You seen all the posters, right?"

"I guess I have. They're hanging on every street in the neighborhood. There's one there. It says it starts today."

The boys examined a brightly-colored poster attached to a telephone pole. *Cole Brothers Circus and Carnival.* It had a picture of a tiger jumping through a fiery hoop; a lady riding a bicycle on a high wire; a pharaoh in a tall head-dress; and a gypsy who wore a dangling hoop earring and whose head looked like it was wrapped in a towel.

"Why'd you go there? It's not open in the morning."

"I didn't have anything to do so I went to see." Emery ran to the telephone pole and put his finger on the gypsy. "See this guy? He talked to me. He called me over to his tent. I made a wish, and he granted it."

Philip's confidence in Emery plummeted.

"He told you to make a wish; you, nobody but you, and he granted it like a genie who popped out of a bottle?"

"Yeah, I wished I could see the circus, and look." With flair, Emery pulled a ticket to the circus from his pocket. "I didn't even have to pay."

Philip studied the ticket. This put things into a different light. With Emery waving the ticket under his nose, he had to believe him.

"How'd you get it? For free, really?"

"Didn't I say how I got it, and didn't I say it was for free?"

"You did. You did. But why'd he pick you?"

"Let me tell you what happened."

CHAPTER TWO

Earlier that day Emery had walked over to see the bustle of preparation going on at Lighthouse Field. Tents were going up; circus people ran to and fro; an occasional horse or elephant walked past. Emery decided to take a closer look. No one paid any attention to him as he walked through the madness, trying to keep out of everyone's way. Then it happened.

"Boy."

Emery paused. He was the only boy he saw.

"You, boy."

Emery turned and saw a gypsy sitting at a small round table outside of a small tent. The gypsy was dressed in a baggy, silky-looking shirt and pants and had a red bandanna wrapped around his head. A big, round, golden earring dangled from his right ear, and he sported a big black mustache.

"Me?" Emery squeaked.

The gypsy didn't answer, but simply crooked a long finger in summons.

Emery felt his heartbeat jump, but he obeyed.

"Sit down," the gypsy said. To Emery's ear it sounded like *seet dowwwn,* and Emery thought he recognized the voice. He did! It sounded like the voice he'd heard in an old movie he and Philip had watched. It sounded like the voice of Count Dracula! Afraid to do anything but what the gypsy demanded, Emery sat on a folding wooden chair near the gypsy.

"I think you can help me," the gypsy said with his frighteningly slow pronunciation.

"M... m... me?"

"If you can help me, I will grant you a wish immediately. Say you can help me."

Behind him Emery heard an elephant trumpet, and Emery wondered how in the world he had ended up in the short space of a minute with a scary-talking gypsy in front of him and a bleating elephant behind him.

"Well, I... I don't know. What... what... what... ?

The gypsy raised a finger to him, and Emery shut up as the gypsy reached under his table and pulled out a creamy glass ball. Emery stared wide-eyed as the gypsy put the ball on the table.

"Stare into the ball," the gypsy ordered. "Stare hard."

Emery glued his eyes to the ball, relieved the gypsy had not ordered him to stare at the gypsy himself.

"You have a wish," the gypsy drawled. "I can see it in the ball. No, do not tell me what it is. The crystal ball will tell me, and because you will help me, I will grant your wish."

Emery peeked up at the gypsy whose eyes were closed as he rubbed his hands across the ball.

"I see it!" the gypsy barked, and Emery jumped and returned his eyes to the ball, not wanting the gypsy to catch him looking anywhere else.

"Now, you may look away. The vision is gone."

Emery shyly returned his eyes to the gypsy.

"You wish to see the circus." The gypsy's voice rose. "I grant you your wish." From somewhere in the folds of his billowing sleeve, the gypsy produced what looked like a ticket. "You may take this to the box office anytime and exchange it for a ticket to the circus. Your wish is granted. Now, you see my power. Now, you see what I can do. Now, you will help me, and if you do, I will grant you three more wishes at the completion of your task."

Emery took the ticket and studied it. It looked like the real thing. And for free!

"What do I have to do?" Emery asked with a quaver in his voice.

"I have a chore for you. You need only do what I ask, and the three wishes are yours."

"Do I have to do it alone?"

The gypsy tilted his head questioningly.

"Two people might be better," Emery argued. "I have a friend. He could help me do whatever it is."

"Bring him to me," the gypsy ordered. "Immediately!"

"Uh, well, okay. I'll go get him." He stood and slipped the ticket into his pocket. "I'll be right back." He took a few steps and turned back. "You'll be here, right?"

The gypsy didn't answer, but simply extended his arm, his crooked finger pointing into the distance.

Emery turned and ran off.

❦ ❦ ❦

"So how about that?" Emery bubbled. "What do you think of that? I showed you the ticket. It's all real."

Philip wanted a free ticket to the circus. What made Emery the lucky one? But it still sounded weird.

"The ticket *looks* real. Did you sit there and make a wish to go to the circus, and he just... *poof...* popped out a ticket?"

"No, I didn't say anything."

"So, you didn't make a wish?"

"No, but I wanted to see the circus."

"But you didn't tell the gypsy that?"

"I guess he could see into my mind through his crystal ball. Oh, man. He read my mind! He's even more powerful than I thought!" A worried look came across Emery's face. "We better watch out what we think when we're around him."

"People can't read minds," Philip said, not entirely sure his statement rang true.

"Then how'd the gypsy know I wanted to go see the circus?"

"I don't know. Everybody wants to go see the circus."

"I don't think so. The old lady who made you lose your ball probably doesn't want to go see the circus."

"She should be *in* the circus; in the Spooky House."

"Philip, you gotta come and meet the gypsy. If he lets you help me, he'll give you three wishes. Imagine what we could do with three wishes."

The possibilities appealed to Philip. "Yeah," he said. "What would you wish for?"

"I don't know. A million dollars. All 100s in every test I ever take. How about you?"

"A million dollars sounds good, but I wouldn't waste a wish on school. How about... how about a new car every year for free when I grow up? Yeah. And muscles."

"Mussels? You eat that snotty-looking seafood thing in the little black shells? Ew! That's disgusting!"

"What snotty seafood thing? Are you crazy? I don't want to eat any snotty-looking seafood?"

"You just said you want it."

"I never said I wanted snotty-looking seafood. I want muscles." Philip stretched out his arms and bent them.

"Ohhhh," said Emery. "Those muscles. Muscles? That's stupid."

"Yeah, well, when I have muscles, and you bother me, I'll use them."

"I give you three wishes, and you're going to muscle me? Forget it. I'll get somebody else to help me then."

Philip knew he'd gone too far. "No, I'm just kidding, Emery. Muscles are good for, you know, doing stuff. Lifting things. And they look good, right?"

Emery gazed doubtfully at Philip. "I guess so. Well, come on. Let's go see the gypsy."

CHAPTER THREE

They hurried toward Lighthouse Field, but slowed down considerably once they entered the grounds.

"Wow!" said Philip. "Everybody's so busy. Is that the guy?"

"Him? Does he look like a gypsy to you?"

"He looks like something."

"He's an Egypt guy, a pharaoh. See the snake thingie on his headpiece? Don't you remember? We saw pictures of them in school this year."

"Oh, yeah. I remember. I like Isis."

"Nothing's open yet. You can't get any."

Philip stopped walking. "I can't get any what?"

"Ices. I like mango."

"You like mango what?"

"Mango ices."

"What are you talking about? Who's mango Isis? They don't have mangos in Egypt."

"Whose mango ices? Anybody's. And what's Egypt have to do with mango ices?"

Philip's voice rose. "There's no mango Isis or banana Isis or apple Isis. There's just Isis."

"There's mango and banana. I've had them. They're good. Especially when it's hot out. I don't think there's apple, though."

"*Argh!*" Philip howled. "Let's start over. The Egypt guy. I said Isis. I didn't say ices."

Emery stared at his friend. "Can you say that again?"

Philip scrooched his mouth together hard, trying to be patient. "I said, I said Isis. I didn't say ices."

"You said ices, but you didn't say ices?"

"Right. Now you got it."

"I got it? I don't even know what I'm *talking* about. Are you feeling all right?"

Philip's voice rose. "We studied Egypt, and we studied Isis. She's like a goddess or something."

"Ohhhh. Isis. You said Isis. I thought you said ices."

Philip nearly screamed. "I did say Isis!"

"I thought you meant ices, like cold stuff in a cup. Mango, remember?"

Philip threw his hands to his head. "Why would I be talking about an Egypt guy and mango ices at the same time?"

Emery shrugged. "Yeah, I thought you *were* talking kind of weird."

"I was *talking* weird? You were *listening* weird."

"Shhhh," Emery cautioned. "Let's go and find the gypsy." They walked a few steps and Emery said, "Now you made me want a mango ice. Look out! Don't step there. Elephant poop."

Philip gritted his teeth and walked in a loop.

A moment later, Emery pointed. "There he is."

Philip saw him. He looked like a real gypsy. The man sat in front of his tent, the small round table next to him, just as Emery had described. When he saw the boys, he sat up straight and beckoned them.

"This is my friend I told you about," Emery said.

"Sit." To Philip, it sounded like *seeet*.

Emery took a second folding chair and put it next to the one he'd sat in earlier. He and Philip sat down.

"So," the gypsy began, "you will do a task for me?"

Philip and Emery turned to one another. Emery turned back to the gypsy.

"I guess so. For three wishes. We each get three wishes," said Emery.

"What! Six wishes. It cannot be done! No! I can grant *three* wishes only. You must share the wishes. Do not waste them. Never again in your life will you have your wishes granted the way I can grant them. Three wishes only are in my power to grant."

Philip and Emery glanced nervously at one another again.

"Well, okay, I guess," Emery said. "What do we have to do?"

The gypsy leaned close to the boys.

"Do you know the word *artifact?*"

"I think so," said Philip. "We learned it in school this year." The word had come up when they studied about Egypt. "It's something valuable from long ago."

"Very good." It sounded to Philip like he said "fairy goot."

"Long ago an artifact was stolen from my very good friend Achmed. There is Achmed."

The boys looked where the gypsy pointed and saw the Egyptian man they'd noticed earlier. He sat outside another tent across from the gypsy's tent, looking their way.

The gypsy continued. "The artifact is very valuable. It has been in Achmed's family since the time of the pyramids, the very time you studied about. Emperor Tutankhamen... no, I should let Achmed tell you about it." The gypsy rose and gestured to Achmed. The boys watched Achmed rise and come slowly forward, still wearing his headpiece.

"Achmed," the gypsy began, "these boys will help you recover your valuable artifact. Everyone, come inside."

Philip and Emery entered the gypsy's tent. The gypsy brought the boys' chairs inside for them, and the boys sat and quickly inspected the place. Small colored lights were strung across the top of the tent. Five large, white, unlit candles sat in different spots in what looked like over-sized ashtrays. A cot and a small side table holding a paperback book and some change sat in a corner of the tent. The gypsy sat on the edge of the cot while Achmed took the one soft chair in the room.

"I told them about the jewels of King Tut stolen from you," the gypsy said.

"Yes, thank you, Bela. Boys, long ago my ancestor Tut, the great pharaoh of Egypt, possessed many jewels, one in particular. After his murder, the possession of the jewels fell to my family, a royal family of Egypt."

Philip glanced at Emery and noticed his eyes were as wide open as his own. The pharaoh was a short man, clean-shaven, who looked about the same age as Bela the gypsy; both a lot older than his father, Philip thought.

"Listen to me, boy," the pharaoh snapped, and Philip spun his head and looked into the pharaoh's eyes. "After centuries and centuries, someone stole those jewels from my family. But now I have traced them to this town... *your* town, and you must help me recover them."

The gypsy interrupted. "He must have the jewels back because one of them has the power!"

"The power!" Achmed repeated.

"Wha... what power?" Philip asked in a small voice.

Achmed turned to Bela. "Should we tell them?"

"Achmed, they deserve to know if they are going help us."

"You are right. Boys, the jewels are in a wooden box. Show them."

Bela the gypsy produced a photograph and handed it to Philip. Emery bent over to look. They saw a plain wooden box the size of a cigar box, with the letters K and T carved into the lid.

King Tut! Philip thought.

Achmed glanced over his shoulder through the tent flaps before whispering, "The jewels are in this box. The box we have traced to the home of an old woman who lives at 1159 Van Kirk Street."

Philip's and Emery's heads spun, and their eyes met. They knew her!

Philip turned back to Achmed. "We know her."

"Excellent! But be warned. One jewel in the box has the power to give the old woman powers; dangerous powers!"

"Powers?" Emery said softly. "What powers? You mean like a witch?"

"Emery, she pointed her finger at me, and my ball went down the sewer," Philip reminded him.

Achmed jumped in. "You see! She has the power, but doesn't know it. If she did to you what you say she did, she is learning her power. If she discovers that her power comes from the scarab in the box, there will be no stopping her."

"The what?" Emery asked.

"The scarab. The scarab."

"What's a scarab?" Philip asked, imagining a many-legged, disgusting looking bug. If any bugs *were* involved, Philip knew he'd count himself out, three wishes or not.

"A scarab is a sacred amulet," Achmed explained, putting his hands together to form a small circle with his fingers to show the size of the amulet.

"Is it alive?" Philip asked.

"Tshhh," Emery hissed. "I thought you studied Egypt. It's like a necklace, you know. The thing that hangs from the necklace."

"Exactly," Bela said. "And you must get it and all the other jewels away from the woman before disaster happens and her power rises. You see how she broke your heart by making your ball go down the sewer."

Philip mumbled, "My heart didn't break. It was just a ball."

"How can *we* do anything?" Emery asked.

"We believe the box is somewhere in her garage," Achmed explained. "You go into her garage and find it. Two boys are much less suspicious than a gypsy and a pharaoh walking through the neighborhood."

"Yes, the box will have a tag with this number on it," Bela added. He took a small ticket from inside his sleeve and showed it to the boys. "6482. Remember that number, and you will be sure you have the right box. Bring that box here, and you will receive three wishes. Think of it. Three wishes all your own." Bela the gypsy turned to Philip. "And now, I will fulfill your wish. Close your eyes; both of you. Ah, I see... I see your wish. Yes, yes, yes!" He reached inside his baggy sleeve and pulled out a circus ticket. "Open your eyes." He handed the ticket to Philip and said, "Your wish is fulfilled. Remember, though, we will be here only until Sunday afternoon. That evening we move on. You have four days. Can we count on you?"

"Yes," Achmed said, leaning forward, "can we?"

The boys' eyes met, and Emery gave a little shrug. Philip shrugged back. Emery looked at Achmed and said, "I guess so."

CHAPTER FOUR

The boys walked in quiet contemplation for a while before Philip spoke.

"Where'd he get the ticket from? I didn't see."

"I didn't see either, but he got mine out of his sleeve. What's pawn mean?"

"You know what a pawn is. The little man in the chess set."

"No, I don't think so."

"Of course it is. You taught me how to play. The whole front line of pieces are pawns. You said so."

"I know *they're* pawns, but there must be another pawn. Did you notice on the ticket the gypsy showed us? With the number? It said pawn on it."

"Oh, right," Philip recalled. "I did see that. Pawn. Pawn. I think my father watches a show… something about pawn. Pawn Stories; something like that. I never watched. I don't know what it's about."

"Ask him," Emery suggested. "Or watch with him."

Philip considered. "No. He'd get suspicious. I already told him most of the shows he watches are stupid. People singing and then getting told how bad they are. News. No. Why don't we just Google it? I don't think we want anybody asking us why we're interested in pawn until we know what it is."

"Good idea. Wanna walk past the old lady's house?"

"Think we should?"

"We're just walking."

Philip considered again.

"Can't hurt, I guess. We've seen her garage. I threw my ball against it before she hexed me."

"You really think she's learning to be a witch? She looks like one."

Philip tried to remember whether the ball he bounced off the garage had hit a crack or... he thought it bounced off his knee, but he couldn't exactly remember.

"All I know is my ball went sailing to the sewer when she pointed her witchy finger at me."

The boys stopped at the corner, paused, and searched each other's eyes. They would have to make a turn onto this street if they wanted to pass by the old woman's house.

"Let's walk on the opposite side of the street of her house, at least," Emery suggested.

That sounded like the safe thing to do, and Philip agreed. They walked along slowly until they were opposite the garage. A wide lawn separated the garage from the old woman's house and the houses behind it. A short driveway separated the garage door from the street. The right side of the garage had a narrow cement walkway which stopped at a regular door in the middle of the garage wall. Low bushes separated the garage from the house next door on that side.

"See the side door?" Philip asked. "I wonder if she keeps it locked."

"If she keeps jewels in it, she probably keeps it locked." Emery walked part of the way into the street and tried to see down the narrow walkway. When he returned to Philip, he said, "The garage door has those four little square windows like a plus sign. If the door's locked, we can bust the window by the doorknob."

"That'll make noise."

"Not much. We can break the window and go away and come back later—in case somebody hears it and comes to investigate right away."

"When should we break the window? And when should we come back?"

"The gypsy said we have until Sunday."

"Look," said Philip, "let's find out what pawn means on a ticket with a number before we do anything."

"Good idea. It might mean atomic radiation or something like that."

"Emery, it's not going to mean atomic radiation."

"I don't mean atomic radiation really. I just mean something bad. Let's leave before she sees us. I don't want her to point at me and send me down the sewer."

Philip wanted to tell Emery how stupid that sounded, yet it could be true, he thought.

Instead, he said, "You go and see what your computer says about pawn, and I'll check mine. I'll come for you after lunch."

Their plan agreed upon, the boys made their way home.

🐦 🐦 🐦

Emery answered Philip's knock on his door, an orange Popsicle in one hand. "What'd you find?"

Philip stared at the treat.

"You want one? We only got orange and only the kind with one stick and not two."

"Sure."

The Popsicle taken care of, Philip asked, "Where's your mom?"

"Upstairs with the babies." Emery had two little sisters, a year apart in age.

"She might hear us."

"Ha! My mother doesn't even hear me when I talk right to her. She's always got a baby in her arms and is talking to herself. My mother had me doing stuff. I didn't get to go on the computer yet. Did you find it?"

"Yeah. A pawnshop is a place you take stuff, and they give you money for it."

"I'd like to take my two sisters to a pawnshop then."

"Not people, dummy. Stuff."

"Like scarabs?"

"Jewelry, sure. I guess. Anyway, Wikipedia says you give the guy the stuff, and he gives you a ticket. If you want your stuff back, you have to pay him more than he gave you. If you don't show up after a while, he keeps whatever you gave him and sells it."

"So the lady has the stuff, and the pharaoh and gypsy have the ticket?"

"Looks like."

"Why don't they give her the ticket and get the box back?"

"Because she's not the pawnshop; she bought the box from the pawnshop. She wants it. It's hers now. Get it?"

"I guess so. So what's it all mean?" Emery asked softly.

"It means they didn't go to buy the box back in time, and the old lady bought the box of jewels and doesn't know about the magical scarab. The gypsy wants it back before she does know and causes trouble. So, should we do it?"

"Get the jewels?"

"No, open a pawnshop. Yes, get the box of jewels."

"Let's go to Mrs. Logan's bushes. We need a plan." Mrs. Logan's house on their block had lots of bushes, and the boys had found a convenient hidey-hole in them. The bushes had grown in a way leaving the boys an igloo-shaped space big enough to sit and even lie down in if they wanted.

"You gotta tell your mother you're going out?" Philip asked.

"She wouldn't hear me if I did. Let's go."

After two hours of arguing and plotting, the boys finally had a plan they agreed on. It was dangerous; it could get them into a world of trouble; it could fall apart and even get them arrested, they thought; but with three wishes on the line, they agreed the attempt was worth the danger, and they would put their plan into operation that very night.

CHAPTER FIVE

"Hi, Dad. How was work?"

Philip's father lowered his newspaper. Dinner had ended, and Philip believed he'd found the right time to get the plan underway.

"How was work? My work?"

"Sure your work. Who else's?"

"You've never asked me before."

Philip shrugged. His father *had* to be difficult.

"A typical day. Nothing particularly noteworthy. And how was your day?"

Ha! The question Philip had been hoping for.

"I won a free circus ticket. Emery and I each won one."

"Really! How so?"

"We were walking around watching them set up the circus and the sideshow, and they picked us out and gave us each a ticket. See?"

Philip waved the ticket in front of his father, who took it and inspected it.

"Very nice."

"Okay if Emery and I go tomorrow night?"

Philip's mother's voice came from behind him.

"You mean alone? Just the two of you?"

"Sure, it's only over at Lighthouse Field. That's not far."

Philip's father interrupted.

"How about I pick you and Emery up afterward so we're sure you get home safely?"

"You don't have to, Dad. We'll be okay."

"No, I agree with your father. He'll pick you up after. Decide where you'll meet." His mother turned and went back to whatever she'd been doing.

Philip's father pointed up and said, "Word has come down. So where shall I meet you, and when?"

Philip had been afraid of this but expected it. He and Emery never imagined they'd be allowed to walk home alone late at night in the dark. They'd figured the circus would last about two hours, and it began at seven-thirty.

"Can you meet us at ten? There's a big cotton candy and peanut stand just as you go into the sideshow part." If his father agreed, he and Emery would have half-an-hour on their own after the circus ended.

"Ten o'clock at the cotton candy booth. I'll be there." His father lifted up his newspaper, and his face disappeared behind it.

Yes! Philip cried silently. He went to the phone and called Emery to tell him their plan was working!

The next day Philip and Emery hung around each other's houses, nervously awaiting the evening. They stayed away from the old woman's house, in case she spent the day rocking on her porch. When they went home for dinner, they promised to meet again at six-fifteen. That's when the toughest part of the plan would kick in.

"You got some rocks?" Philip asked as he and Emery walked speedily toward Van Kirk Street.

Emery patted his pocket. "I got 'em."

"It's awful light out."

"Don't worry. It won't take us long. Once we break the window, we head on over to the circus real quick. She can't get a window fixed at night. No glass-fixing store will be open. We come back after the circus when it's dark, go in, and find the box. 6482. You got the flashlight, right?"

Philip produced a small flashlight two inches long and as thick as two of his fingers.

"You sure it works?" Emery asked. "Turn it on."

Philip flicked the switch, and the light came on.

"I even brought an extra battery in case the one inside burns out. I don't know how long it's been in there."

The boys quieted as they turned onto Van Kirk Street. When they approached the old woman's house, they crossed the street, angling toward the bushes next to the garage. When they reached the bushes, they hunkered down, hoping no one could see them. From where they knelt, they could see the old woman's house clearly.

"Give me the rocks," Philip whispered. "You be the lookout. Okay, I'm gonna break the window." He stood and took a step.

"Witch! Window!" Emery whispered in a panic.

Philip paused and turned to Emery. "Which window? What do you mean which window? The window right there; the one in the door by the doorknob."

"Witch! Door!" Emery cried louder in even greater panic.

"Which door? What is wrong with you? There's only one door. Right there. Right there. You see another door?"

"She's coming?"

"Who's coming?"

"Stop talking. The witch is coming. Hide!"

Philip peeked around the garage so he could see what Emery saw—the old woman hobbling across her lawn in their direction.

"Oh!" Philip cried. "Why didn't you tell me?"

"I did tell you! She looked out the window; I said witch, window. She came out the door; I said witch, door. You didn't listen. You kept talking and asking stupid questions."

"You didn't make it clear. You said witch window, and I thought you said which window."

"I *did* say witch, window! Never mind now. We gotta hide."

Philip looked around. "We have to crawl further under. Go get under more. Go, under the bushes."

The boys dove deeper into the bushes and wriggled on their stomachs as far as the bushes permitted. They faced the garage and breathed as quietly as they knew how.

They saw the long swishy black dress of the woman and heard her fussing with the side door of the garage. They heard her talk to herself.

"Where did I put... did I drop it?"

They saw the woman's legs go back the way they came. Emery poked his head out of the bush.

"Philip, the door's open. She left it open. Come on, quick."

Philip crawled forward.

"You mean go into the garage now?"

"Yeah, before she comes back. Why are you always talking so much?"

Emery scampered into the garage, and Philip followed him. They were brought up short and stared in amazement. The garage was packed so full of stuff they had only the smallest space to stand in. There were cardboard boxes full of magazines and books; wooden boxes filled with smaller boxes; shelves full of glasses and vases and little statues and old clothes.

"I hear her voice," said Philip. "She's coming back. There's no room to hide in here."

"Climb up on the boxes and get behind the rocking chair."

The boys scrambled awkwardly over boxes and chairs and tables and crammed themselves behind an old wooden rocking chair. The old woman entered the garage, and the boys stared down at her, hoping she wouldn't turn their way. They watched as the old woman unloaded a brown shopping bag. She pulled out two small statues which she unwrapped from the paper protecting them and squeezed them onto a shelf she could barely reach. She pulled out two big piles of magazines and tossed them over some boxes onto a pile of other magazines that peeked out over the boxes.

"Ahhh," the old woman began in her creaky voice, "there you are my little pretty."

Philip stomach danced. He hoped he wasn't the *little pretty* she had discovered. He watched her take a small round mirror, very decorated and with a short handle, and lay it gently inside an open box at her right shoulder. The old woman looked over her stash, and Philip scrooched down. The woman gave a satisfied chuckle and left the garage, closing the door behind her.

"She's gone," Philip whispered. "Let's get down before we start knocking things over."

The boys made their careful way back to the floor.

"At least we didn't have to break any windows," Emery whispered.

"We better be able to get out of here," Philip said nervously.

"Go try the door."

Philip slid between boxes and things to the door. Terror shot through him when the doorknob refused to turn. "We're locked in!" he cried.

Emery peeked over his shoulder.

"Try the little button. Turn the button."

Philip gave the button in the center of the doorknob a small turn. When he tried the doorknob this time, it worked.

"There, see. We can get out."

Philip breathed a long sigh of relief, eager for this part of the plan to be over with. "Let's look for the box. I don't like being in here."

"In all this junk? Where will we look?"

Philip thought a moment.

"It probably won't be with all the magazines and newspapers. It's not on the tables or chairs or shelves we can see. Look in those boxes where she put the mirror. Maybe that's where she puts her fancy stuff."

Emery slid around Philip and started looking through the box where the woman had put the mirror.

"There's a big box over there," said Philip. "I'll climb up on these magazines..."

"I see a couple boxes on the bottom," Emery interrupted over his shoulder.

"You see any numbers on them?"

"I see a tag, but it's tucked in between other boxes. Come help me."

Philip jumped down from the stack of magazines. The pile wobbled as he jumped, and Philip held his breath until the magazine pile steadied.

"What do you want me to do?" Philip asked.

"I can't reach down far enough. Let me on your shoulders."

Philip didn't much like the idea of Emery stepping on him. "Why don't you get one of those chairs?"

"We pull out a chair, and everything'll fall down. Come on. You want to see the circus or what? We're wasting time."

Philip did want to see the circus, so he bent down, and Emery stood on his back.

"Okay, stand up slow now," Emery ordered.

Philip staggered to his feet with Emery telling him to go right and left and stand up and bend over.

"Stop telling me what to do," Philip puffed, out of breath from moving Emery around.

"Be still. I can reach now."

"Tell me what you're doing."

"There's a tag on the string. I'm trying to pull it... I got it. 6482! It's the box."

"Can you get it out?"

"Let me get... wait... here hold this."

Emery reached a box down to Philip. Philip could only move his eyes since Emery's ankles were clamped tightly against his ears.

"What am I supposed to do with this?" Philip asked, impatient with Emery's giving him so many orders.

"It was in the way. Here, hold this one, too."

"Another one?"

"Here, one more."

"I can't hold so many!"

"Take it," Emery ordered.

Philip balanced the two boxes Emery had already passed him against his chest and took the third one.

"I got it!" Emery cried. "I got it. Kneel down again."

"It's hard to kneel down without my hands."

"Don't use your hands, just use your knees."

"I gotta balance. You're making me wobble."

"Hey, come on. Easy. Now you're making *me* wobble."

Philip managed to get one knee on the floor, and when he did, Emery hopped off. He stood in front of Philip and held out the tag. It said *Riley's Pawnshop* and had the number 6482 clearly printed on it.

"We got it," said Emery triumphantly. "Let's get out of here."

Philip indicated the three boxes he still held. "What about these?"

Emery frowned. "I guess we better put them back where they were so the old lady doesn't get suspicious." Emery put the box he held on the ground. "Kneel down again."

"How about you kneel down this time?" Philip said hotly.

"I know where the boxes go. You don't. Kneel down. Don't always be arguing."

Philip had a hundred reasons why Emery should do the kneeling down this time, but it would take forever, he knew, to convince his friend, and he didn't want to take the time.

Finally, Philip grumbled, "Do it fast."

"Fast as you can kneel down."

Emery replaced the boxes the boys didn't want and climbed down. Philip picked up the box they did want.

"Let's look inside," he said.

Emery nodded, and Philip lifted the lid.

"Wow!" Philip said softly. All kinds of jewelry filled the box. Lots of colored stones, red, blue, yellow, green, white, decorated the jewelry.

"Where's the magic scarab? See it?" Emery asked.

"How do I know which one's a scarab? Anyway, we have no time for looking. Open the door."

Emery opened the door and reset the little knob before he closed it again.

"Uh oh," Emery said and pointed. "Get back." The old woman sat on her porch rocking.

"Here, you take it," said Philip, handing Emery the box. "You keep it."

"We can't walk out there carrying the box. She'll see and do her pointing thing, and we'll both end up down the sewer. Look, let's hide the box in the bushes. If we take it now, one of her neighbors may see us with the box and tell her about it. We were going to come back here tonight anyway after we broke the window. We'll come back when it's dark and get the box. We'll have time. Then we can hide it someplace closer to the circus, and tomorrow we can deliver it to the gypsy."

"Okay. Shove it in there."

Philip got on his knees.

"Shove it in as far as it can go. We don't want anybody to find it before we come back."

Philip got to his feet.

"Let's go through the bushes and come out further down," Philip suggested. "And look out for nosy neighbors."

Emery peeked around the garage. "She's still there. Let's climb through."

The boys pushed their way through the bushes and came back onto the sidewalk well down the block. A man dragging his trash can to the curb waved to them, and they returned the wave. They looked back and saw the old lady still rocking. They glanced nervously at one another and headed off to see the circus.

CHAPTER SIX

The boys enjoyed the circus, especially the motorcycles that roared around inside a giant ball, just missing each other as they zipped in and out and up and down in wild circles. When, at the end of the show, the man flew out of the cannon and sailed across the whole circus tent into a big net, Philip and Emery scooted. They knew they needed to beat the crowd leaving the tent. They had only twenty-four minutes before they had to meet Philip's father.

"Make sure we don't run into your father as we leave," Emery said, trying to keep up. An elephant walked in front of them, and the boys paused outside the tent of the gypsy. They watched a woman step outside, pause, and pat the front of her dress. She spun in a circle, looking around on the ground. The elephant passed, and the boys hurried on to Van Kirk Street.

"Oh, no," Philip said. "Look, she's on her porch."

"Yeah, but it's dark. We can get the box without her seeing. Go ahead."

Philip turned to his friend.

"*We* can get it. *I* should go ahead?"

"Yeah. You know where you put the box, not me."

Philip looked for a way to argue, but Emery had him again.

Emery went on, "I'll keep an eye on the old lady."

"If she comes, you say *here comes the witch.* Okay?" Philip got down on his knees.

"Right. Here comes the witch."

Philip leaped up.

"What are you doing?" Emery asked. "Get back down there."

"You said *here comes the witch.* Is she coming?"

"No, I was just practicing. She's still rocking."

"Well, why did you say *here comes the witch* then?"

"Will you get the box, for Pete's sake?"

"Don't say anything unless she's really coming."

"I won't. Go."

Philip got back onto his knees and crawled forward. He took out his little flashlight and shot its beam into the bushes. He found the box and pulled it out.

"Philip, she stood up," Emery whispered.

Philip got to his feet, and together they peeked around the garage.

"She's lifting her arm," Philip said with a shaky voice. "She can feel we have the box! She knows! She knows! She's gonna put us down the sewer!"

"Listen!"

In the distance, the boys heard a siren.

"You think she can call the police by lifting her arm?" Emery asked softly.

"I don't know. I don't know."

Headlights and sirens turned onto Van Kirk Street. The boys stood frozen in fear as two police cars raced by.

"They missed us," Emery said. "Maybe the old lady's arm is crooked and her aim is off. Run before they come back."

Philip hurried away, Emery at his shoulder.

Two blocks later they slowed, and Emery asked, "Where'll we put the box this time? In Mrs. Logan's bushes?"

"We don't have time. We better find a place around here where it's dark. Near the circus there'll be lots of lights and lots of people. How about there?"

Philip indicated a corner store, closed at the moment, but which had an unlit outdoor staircase along the side wall. He walked to the staircase and put the box under the first step. Then he pulled two trashcans under the staircase to block the view of anyone going by.

"I guess it's okay there," said Emery. "But we better come by first thing in the morning when the store opens and get it."

"Come get me as early as you can."

"I will, but the circus doesn't open until noon."

"We'll get the box and take it with us. At noon we'll go and give it to the gypsy."

"Okay. Let's go meet your father. How much time we got?"

Philip checked his watch. "Seven minutes."

The boys ran back toward the circus grounds.

The next morning, Philip and Emery found the box exactly where they'd left it, and Philip put the box inside a plastic bag he'd thought to bring along.

"People will think we went to the supermarket," he reasoned with Emery.

"Now what?"

"Now we can hide in Mrs. Logan's bushes until it's time to leave for the circus."

"Good. We can't be too careful. Three wishes! This will be so great."

The boys slipped into their hideout and sat down, the valuable plastic bag between them.

"Did you think more about what you'll do with your wish?" Emery asked dreamily.

"What do you mean my *wish*? We have three wishes."

"Yeah, but you can't divide three in half."

"So you get two wishes?"

"I found the wishes, didn't I? The gypsy gave them to me first."

"So what? I did everything you did. I did *more*. *You* got to stand on me; *I* didn't stand on you. *I* crawled under the bush to hide the box, not you; *I* got the box back out, not you; *I* brought the plastic bag, not you. I did *everything!*"

"Yeah, but the gypsy gave me the wishes first, not you," Emery repeated. "Anyway, a plastic bag's nothing."

"But you were *afraid* to do it yourself. You wouldn't have *any* wishes if I didn't do everything."

"And you wouldn't have any wishes if I didn't let you know about it. Besides, you didn't do everything," Emery replied. "I found the box in the garage, didn't I?"

"Because you were standing on me! If you didn't stand on me, you wouldn't have found the box. Let's split one wish."

"Split it? How?"

"Let's ask for something we can share. Like let's ask for a million dollars. Then you can take half, and I can take half."

Emery considered. "How can we carry half of a million dollars into the house?"

Philip didn't respond.

"Well?" Emery insisted.

"I don't know. Let me think." A few quiet minutes went by. "How about we wish that when we're twenty-one years old, a *million* dollars shows up in each of our bank accounts. We should have bank accounts of our own by then, don't you think?"

"Yeah. Yeah! Great idea. How about your other wish?"

More quiet minutes went by as the two boys thought things over.

"How about you?" Philip asked. "And don't waste it on something dumb like getting good marks in school."

"I am going to wish that I never hear my sisters cry again. Or even talk to me when they learn to talk. That would be *great*! That would keep me happy until I was twenty-one, and then the money will show up in my bank account to keep me happy after that."

Philip nodded. It made sense to him.

"Now you," said Emery.

"I think I'll wish that I never even *get* a brother or sister. That way there'll be nobody to bother me the way your sisters bother you. Then *I'll* be happy until the money shows up."

"Great idea," Emery agreed. The boys lapsed into dreamy silence as they contemplated their glorious futures, and the minutes slipped by.

The gypsy and the pharaoh sat talking outside the gypsy's tent when Philip and Emery arrived. The two men rose in anticipation.

Philip held out the plastic bag. "We got it," he said proudly.

"Shhhh!" the gypsy counseled. "Come inside."

The boys followed the men into the tent. Philip handed over the box. The gypsy took it out of the plastic bag and shared a smile with the pharaoh. He opened the box and ran his fingers over the jewelry. He took another piece of jewelry from somewhere in his sleeve and put it into the box before closing the lid and sliding the box under his cot.

"You did well," said the gypsy, pronouncing well as *vell.*

"Very well," the pharaoh agreed.

"Can we have our wishes now?" Emery asked.

"Your wishes? Ah, yes of course," said the gypsy. He stepped outside and came back in holding his creamy glass ball. "Place your hands on the crystal ball," he said slowly. "Close your eyes."

Philip and Emery obeyed. Philip thought he heard a snort and a gurgle from the two men, but he didn't dare open his eyes. He listened to the gypsy say words in a strange language.

"There you are," said the gypsy. "You may open your eyes. The three wishes are yours. But you had better listen to Achmed. He has a story to tell you."

"A story?" Philip repeated.

"I had better take the boys to my tent," said Achmed softly.

"They would be safer that way," Bela agreed.

"S... safer?" Emery sputtered.

"Come with me." Achmed rose, and the boys followed him across the midway to his tent. He lifted the flap, and the boys entered. Achmed followed them inside, dropping the flap behind him. The tent was dark with the flap closed, so Achmed put two tall candles on a small square table and lit them. The candle flames sent wriggling shadows dancing across the tent walls and along the floor.

"Sit," Achmed ordered. "Sit and listen carefully."

CHAPTER SEVEN

"What do we have to listen to?" Philip asked in a hushed voice.

The pharaoh stared briefly at Philip with his large, round eyes before pulling a chair up near the boys.

"A wish is a powerful thing. It cannot be taken lightly. You and you now have three wishes. Before you do anything with them I must tell you of people I once knew. They, like you, performed an important service for the gypsy. They, like you, received three wishes in return. They were a poor couple who could not survive without the help of their grown son, who worked in a factory and always gave them some money to help them pay their bills and buy food. The old couple talked for days about what they should do with their three wishes, and do you know what they decided?"

The pharaoh stared at the boys, waiting for an answer.

"No," Philip squeaked.

The pharaoh's eyes widened. "They... chose... money! They wanted to relieve their son of the burden of supporting them, so they wished for a lot of money. One minute after the man spoke their wish aloud, the telephone rang. The old man answered it. The president of the company for which his son worked was on the line telling him that his son had fallen into the machinery and was no more. He was gone forever." The pharaoh's voice had risen steadily as he related the fate of the young man. "Do you know what that means?" he asked.

Emery cleared his throat. "Uh, it means he died?"

"Yes! But then the president of the company said something that sent horrible chills through the heart of the old man. He said the company's insurance policy would pay them five hundred thousand dollars because of the accident! They had gotten the money they'd wished for! When the old man reported the horrible news to his wife, his wife nearly went insane. *We wished our son's death. We killed our own son,* she moaned. She and her husband were torn apart by the realization that their wish for wealth came true at the expense of the life of their only son."

The gypsy paused, and Philip reminded himself to breathe.

"What then?" Emery whispered.

"They still had two wishes, and the old woman knew exactly what to wish for. She wanted her son back. The old man agreed. If the first wish came true, so would the second one. That very night they sat in the dark at their dining room table. This time the woman spoke the wish out loud. *I wish to have my son back.* They waited. The night was quiet; as quiet as a tomb. Only eight minutes later they heard the sound of something being dragged through the street toward their house. They heard a scraping sound and then a pause. Scrape. Pause. Something approached their front door! Louder and louder; nearer and nearer came the scraping sound. Then it stopped. Right outside their door! Then RAP! One solitary knock on their door. The old woman leaped up. *My son,* she screamed. RAP! Another lonely knock. The woman started to the door, but her husband was wiser. He realized what his wife did not. Her wish had come true! Too true. He grabbed his wife and would not let her go near the door. The wife screamed to be let free to see her son again. RAP!"

The boys jumped as the pharaoh gave another loud knock on the door.

"The old man wrapped his arms around his wife and screamed at the top of his lungs, *I wish my son back where he came from. Immediately!* The old woman began to beat at her husband, not realizing the wisdom of his choice. They froze as the scraping sound again began, this time moving away. Soon, the noise faded into nothingness."

The pharaoh stared at the boys and nodded his head slowly.

"Do you know why the man wished his son away?"

Emery and Philip shook their heads silently.

"Remember, he had fallen into a machine. He was terribly hurt. He was dead. *A dreadful dead person had come back to life and stood knocking on their front door!* The old man had figured out what happened and wisely sent the son away. So, my dear children, you must be very careful what you wish for. Because wishes... do... come... true."

The pharaoh stood and walked to the tent entrance. He opened the flap, and sunlight flooded in, making the boys wince.

"Go now. And I wish you the wisdom of the old man."

Philip and Emery stood and, like two people in trances, stepped out of the tent and onto the midway. They walked two blocks before Emery broke the silence.

"You want to make your wish first?" he asked.

"What? Me? No. You can go first."

"I don't think I'm ready yet."

"Let's go sit in Mrs. Logan's bushes," Philip suggested. "I'm all out of breath, and I didn't even do anything."

"Good idea," Emery agreed. "We better think about this."

The boys hurried back to their hideout in Mrs. Logan's bushes. They looked at each other questioningly. Finally, Philip spoke.

"Maybe we shouldn't ask for money. You see what happened to those other people when they asked for money."

"You don't think saying the things we wanted this morning was like really making the wishes, and it counted, do you?"

"How could it count for real? We didn't even have the three wishes yet."

"I wish we knew about this story before we gave the box back."

"Emery!" Philip screamed. "You just made a wish!"

"I did? No, I didn't. Oh, no. I did. I take it back; I take it back," Emery cried looking up toward the sky.

The boys waited. They didn't know for what, but they waited.

"I don't think your wish counted," Philip said softly. "If it did... if it did, we'd already know the story before the pharaoh told us."

"But we know the story now. How do we know we didn't know it before he told us?"

"Because."

"Because what?"

"Because I still remember being surprised by the story. If we knew the story before the pharaoh told it to us, I wouldn't have been surprised."

"Oh, yeah. Me, too. I guess you're right. We gotta be careful." Emery paused. "How do you think the money would come if we wished for it?"

"I don't even *want* to think about it. Let's forget money until we figure out how to get it safely."

"We could wish for money and say it has to come without anybody getting hurt."

"That would be two wishes."

"We have three."

"Yeah, but maybe you can't make two wishes at the same time. Maybe if you do, only the first one counts."

That silenced Emery.

Philip had another thought. "What about your wish about your sisters? That you wouldn't hear them crying. Suppose your wish made you deaf, or you had an accident, and your ears got chopped off. Then you wouldn't hear them."

Emery's eyes bugged. "My ears got chopped off!" He reached up and grabbed onto them. "Yeah, well how about you? Not having any brothers or sisters to bother you? Suppose that came true because..."

"Never mind. Never mind. I don't want to hear it."

The boys fell silent again.

Emery had an idea. "Maybe we should just wish for a new comic book or something simple."

"Seems like an awful waste of a wish. We could *buy* a new comic book. A comic book's nothing."

The boys didn't stay in Mrs. Logan's bushes much longer because everything they thought of frightened them. Every wish they discussed seemed to lead to disaster. When they exited the bushes, they headed for the playground. They joined in a game of baseball, but they didn't enjoy themselves very much. Afterwards, they stopped into Emery's house, but the babies were fussing, so they quickly left and went to Philip's quiet house.

"Enjoying your summer?" Philip's mother asked them. Philip could see she was getting ready to go out.

"Yeah, so much," Philip responded gloomily. "Where are you going?"

"Walking over to the library. Want to come?"

"No, we'll stay here."

"Okay. Your father will be home soon. Emery, would you like to stay for dinner? I'll make hamburgers if you do."

"Stay, Emery," Philip advised.

"Sure. Thanks," Emery said without much enthusiasm.

"I'll be back soon." The boys watched Philip's mother leave the house.

"Now what?" Emery asked.

"Why don't we Google *wishes* and see what it says. Maybe it'll show how to make a safe wish."

"Yeah," Emery said hopefully. "Maybe it'll tell us if we can make two wishes at the same time." They went upstairs to Philip's computer and began their research.

Philip's father came upstairs as the boys were shutting down the computer.

"Is Mom home yet?" Philip asked.

"She came in right behind me. Where'd she go?" his father answered.

"She went to the library. We're having hamburgers for dinner. Emery's staying."

"Ah, that's nice. How are you Emery?"

"I wish I was better."

Philip jabbed Emery with his elbow.

"Why what's wrong?" Philip's father asked.

"Nothing. I'm okay."

"Oh, your mother is paging me. See you at dinner."

"You just wasted another wish. You wished you were better. Don't be saying *I wish* anything," Philip scolded. "Where's your brain?"

"I wish I knew."

"Emery!" Philip screamed.

"Oh, sorry, sorry."

"Uh, do you feel better?"

"No."

"Good."

"Good? It's good I don't feel better?"

"Yeah. It means the wish didn't come true, so it didn't count."

"Oh, yeah, right. But I still don't like what the computer said about wishes. It was like wishes were always make-believe and only in stories."

"I know. I know. Aladdin and Snow White."

"And why did they mention a monkey's paw? What's a monkey got to do with anything?"

"How do I know," Philip said in irritation. An unsettling suspicion had begun to nag at him. "Do you think... you think the gypsy really *can* grant wishes?"

"He could if he was in a story."

"Well, he's *not* in a story, Emery. Maybe we should try an easy wish—an official wish—and we could see whether it comes true or not. Something safe."

"Well, I'm hungry." Emery tilted his head up and in a haunted house, echo-y voice said, "I wish for dinner now."

Philip's mother's voice came from downstairs.

"Come on down, boys. The hamburgers are cooking."

Philip and Emery looked at each other.

"It came true," Emery said softly.

"Maybe not. Why'd you waste a wish on something that was going to happen anyway? Now we don't know if it was the wish or just plain old dinnertime."

"But I said *now,* and it was *now.*"

"It might have been now, anyway," Philip argued, his voice rising. "You shouldn't have said now then."

"I didn't say now then. I only said now. Something *made* me say now then, though. If I said now now, it would be too late."

"You wouldn't *say* now now after my mother already said dinner's ready! What are you talking about! Oh, never mind. Let's go eat."

CHAPTER EIGHT

When Philip and Emery entered the kitchen, they smelled the hamburgers and heard them sizzling. Philip's mother poured a steaming pot of baked beans into a bowl, and Philip's dad poured grape juice into four glasses. A plate of lettuce leaves and sliced tomatoes sat on the kitchen table next to a bottle of ketchup. A few moments later everyone sat around the table digging in.

"What till I tell you what I bumped into on the way back from the library," Philip's mom said after dabbing at her mouth with a napkin. "Over on Van Kirk Street."

"Don't you mean *who?*" Philip's father asked.

"No, I mean what."

Mid-bite of his hamburger Philip paused and looked across the table at Emery, who had stopped chewing, even though his mouth was full. Van Kirk Street.

"Police cars and an hysterical old woman. You know the one who lives alone in the tan house? Mrs. Healy's her name."

"The one who's always on her porch?" answered Philip's father.

"Yes. Well, she was standing on the lawn by her garage with two policemen in the middle of a big crowd. Naturally, I *had* to see what was going on. She claimed she was robbed. Somebody took a box of jewelry from her. The front door of her house was open. Good grief. Even from where I stood I could see there was no room in the house for the police to go in. No wonder they had to talk on the lawn."

"What do you mean?" Philip's father asked.

Philip and Emery had started chewing again, but very slowly so they could listen very intently.

"Junk. Junk everywhere. I heard people talking. They already knew."

"Knew what?"

"How she hoarded things. One woman, who told me her name was Mrs. Faraday, said she'd visited Mrs. Healy lots of times, and there was no room inside the house to move around. Just the narrowest path from room to room. And Mrs. Healy always moved her rocking chair indoors to a space by the front door so she could sleep in it because all the bedrooms were floor to ceiling with junk."

Philip swallowed and asked a question. "What's a hoarder?"

"I just told you," his mother answered. "A pack rat. Somebody who collects things and keeps them and never gets rid of anything. Finally, the house is so filled up with the things the person collected, and there's no room left inside for the person."

"Oh, like her garage," said Emery. Philip shot him an angry look.

Philip's father frowned. "You've been in her garage?"

"Oh, no, no," Philip sputtered. "We were... were bouncing a ball, and it hit something and rolled behind the garage. We looked in the window. The garage has a window. It's all filled up with stuff, too."

"I'm not surprised," said Philip's mother. "How can anyone live that way?"

"Get back to the story," Philip's father suggested. "What did the police do?"

"I heard one policeman ask how she could tell something was missing, and she said she knew exactly where she put everything. Somebody got into her garage, she said, and took a box with jewelry in it. The policemen started shooing people away, but Mrs. Faraday told me that she was the first person Mrs. Healy called when she missed the jewelry, and she advised her to phone the police. It's a wonder she could find the phone to make the call. Seems Mrs. Healy bought things from yard sales, pawn shops, junk stores, anywhere she could find something for sale. She bought the box of jewelry somewhere, and somehow somebody made off with it. So she claims, anyway."

Philip and Emery exchanged another glance at the mention of pawn shops, but their stomachs hit the floor at Philip's mom's next sentence.

"The old woman swears she's seen two young boys hanging around her house."

"When did the jewelry go missing?" asked Philip's dad.

"Last night, I guess. Seems Mrs. Healy saw the box yesterday, but it was missing today."

"Two young boys, eh? Good thing you two were at the circus last night." Philip's father smiled as if he were making a joke. "No one can suspect you two."

"Ha, yeah. Right, Dad. Good thing," Philip said, trying hard to smile back in a normal manner.

The topic changed, and the boys hurried through their dinners. They knew from the looks they gave each other they had to talk.

"Okay if we go over Emery's a while? Still lots of daylight left," Philip said.

"Sure, go ahead. Your mother and I will clean up here. Maybe we'll take a nice walk later, honey?"

Philip's mother smiled in response, and the boys pushed their chairs back and left the house. They walked and talked.

Philip grumbled, "A gypsy, a pharaoh, a dead guy who visits his parents, and now a pack rat hoarder."

Emery threw his arms out and said, "How could the old lady know the box was missing? What'd she do? Climb up on things like a mountain goat and check? She's gotta be like a hundred years old."

"She saw us, too. Does she know you?"

"I don't think so, but she knows you. She called your house, right?"

Philip's stomach spun in great circles.

"Before, yeah. But she didn't call my house yet for this."

"Maybe she saw two boys but couldn't see who. We did try to hide, you know."

"Boy, I hope so."

"Don't worry. She would have called your house already if she knew it was you."

"Suppose the police ask other houses if they saw two boys. Other people might have seen us. They might know us. We weren't trying to hide from the other people. And our fingerprints!! Emery, did we touch anything in the garage?"

"Touch anything? We touched *everything*! We both touched the doorknob before we left."

"Oh, Emery. We're sunk if the police really investigate."

"They will investigate. They'll have to. What are we gonna do?"

They'd reached Emery's house, but they kept walking. They could take no chance of being overheard by any grownups.

"Oh, man," Emery groaned. "I wish the old lady had her box back, and I hope the stupid gypsy and the pharaoh get arrested."

"If *they* don't, *we* might. Our fingerprints, remember?"

Emery had a thought. "If the police come to arrest us, we can tell them about the gypsy and the pharaoh."

"Emery, you think anybody's going to believe we were so stupid to believe we'd get three wishes if we robbed the old lady? Besides, the circus is leaving day after tomorrow."

"You sure the wishes are fakes? I got a circus ticket wish come true. I wished for dinner *now,* and your mother called us down right away."

"We already talked about that. Forget wishes. We have to find some way to get the box back to the old lady so the police stop looking for us and before they check for fingerprints or ask if anybody else in the neighborhood saw me and you."

"How?"

"You tell me how."

"No, you tell me how."

"I can't tell you how. I don't know how."

"I can't tell you how, either. I don't know how, too."

Emery often made Philip's stomach tighten up, and this was one of those times. They walked a while in silence before Philip came up with a meager idea.

"We still have a day and a half. Let's think of something when we go to sleep tonight."

Emery frowned. "How can we think when we're asleep?"

"We don't think when we're asleep. What's wrong with you? Before we fall asleep, we lay in bed and think when we're *awake.*"

"Oh. I thought you meant we'd *dream* an answer."

"How could we dream an answer? Tell me, how? How could you think I meant we'd dream an answer?"

"Stop yelling."

Philip rubbed his stomach to quiet it.

"Let's just go home," Philip said. "Come for me tomorrow morning. We gotta think of something."

The boys finished their walk and separated, Philip deciding he'd better go to bed early so he'd have plenty of time to think.

CHAPTER NINE

Saturday morning found Philip and Emery walking the streets, grumpy with one another after a night of tossing and turning in bed, looking for a way out of their dilemma.

"Maybe," Emery offered, "we should think up a story and stick to it. We were at the circus, and then we met your father, and that's that."

"And when they ask us how our fingerprints got on the jewelry box and in the old lady's garage? Go on. Finish the story."

Emery couldn't.

"Look," said Philip, "we gotta do something to get the jewelry box back to the lady so there's no need for any investigation."

Emery stopped walking.

"Philip! Let's tell the police where the jewelry box is. In the gypsy's tent!"

"Good, you go tell them. I'll wait for you in Mrs. Logan's bushes and never come out again."

"No, on the telephone."

"The telephone?"

"Sure. We call them and tell them where the jewelry box is, only we don't say who we are. They get the jewelry box, arrest the gypsy and the pharaoh, and they don't even have to worry about fingerprints or anything. The gypsy doesn't know who we are really. Just two kids."

Philip saw possibilities.

"You know, Emery, sometimes you get good ideas. Let's do it."

"Okay, you go home and call them."

"What! I can't call them. My parents are home. They can't hear me call the police and tell them about stolen jewelry. You go home and call them."

"I can't. My mom's always there. She doesn't hear much when I talk to her, but she'd hear that. Guaranteed. That's how parents are. They hear what you don't want them to hear and don't hear the other stuff you tell them."

Philip couldn't argue with that.

"I told my mother I needed a cell phone," Emery grumbled.

"That idea's dead then," said Philip, his spirits plummeting.

"How about one of those old fashioned phones," Emery suggested.

"What old fashioned phone?"

"The kind on the street you drop money into."

"Where's one of them?"

"There's one near the school."

"What, the one without the thing you put to your ear? What good's that?"

"There gotta be others. Let's find one."

The boys walked to the supermarket and along the stores lining the small outdoor mall attached to the supermarket. They found one phone, but when Emery put the receiver to his ear he heard nothing.

"I think it's dead," he reported. Philip put the receiver to his own ear and agreed.

"Wasn't there one by the corner store where we hid the box?"

Emery thought back. "Yeah, on the side wall. You think it might work?"

"Let's go and see."

The boys raced to the store, and when they arrived, they gave two people walking by a chance to pass.

"Go try it," Philip said.

Emery put the receiver to his ear.

"It's buzzing like a real phone."

Philip read the instructions and said, "Put in two quarters and call the police."

"You sure we're allowed to do this. Call the police. I only know 911; not the real number."

"We have no choice. Make the call real quick so they can't complain about it."

Emery hung up the phone and pulled a dollar out of his pocket.

"This is all I got."

Philip checked his own pocket and pulled out a dime, two nickels and a penny.

"Get change," Philip suggested, pointing to the store. "Four quarters."

Emery hustled inside the store but returned with a glum look on his face.

"What?" Philip asked.

"He won't give me any change. Says I gotta buy something."

"So go buy something! What'd you come back for? Go. Go."

Philip gave Emery an encouraging little shove, and Emery headed back inside the store. He returned a moment later, the same glum look on his face.

"What now?" Philip cried in exasperation.

"The cheapest thing is a pack of gum, but it's sixty cents. I won't have enough to make the phone call."

Philip dug in his pocket and turned his dime over to Emery.

"Take this. If you spend sixty cents and give him your dollar and my dime, you'll get fifty cents back. Make sure it's two quarters."

Emery took the dime and started off. He turned the corner, but came right back around the corner and walked toward Philip.

"That was fast."

"I didn't go in. What kind of gum you want? They have..."

"Any kind," Philip shouted. "Just go."

"Sheesh. Just asking," Emery grumbled.

When Emery returned, he had an open pack of gum and two quarters. He chewed noisily.

"You opened the gum already?" Philip cried. "You couldn't wait until after the phone call?"

Emery shrugged. "Want a piece?"

"No. Call."

Emery slipped the gum into his pocket and lifted the receiver.

"Disguise your voice," Philip suggested. "And make it quick."

Emery dropped the quarters in the slot and dialed 911.

"Yes, what is your emergency?" came a voice in Emery's ear.

Emery stuffed his tongue in the back of his mouth to change his voice.

"Go to the gypsy and pharaoh, and you'll find the stolen jewels. Ha, yes you will." And he hung up.

Philip slapped his two hands against his forehead.

"What?" Emery asked.

"You didn't tell them what jewels, what gypsy, or what pharaoh. They won't know what you're talking about. And what was *ha, yes you will?* You sounded ridiculous. Like a kid playing a trick"

"You said to make it quick."

"Yeah, but not so quick you sound like a moron. Let's get out of here."

Philip started running, and Emery followed along. Philip didn't stop until he and Emery nestled safely in Mrs. Logan's bushes.

"What were we running for?" Emery asked, out of breath.

Philip glared at Emery. "You know the police don't want people joking when they call them. You sounded like you were making fun of them. *Ha! Yes you will.* Really? They probably can tell where the call came from, and they might go see who made it."

"Oh," was all Emery could think to say. "Now what?"

"Now, we gotta get the box ourselves and give it back to the lady."

Emery's head sailed to the rear in amazement.

"Get the box from the gypsy's tent?"

"I was thinking... when we were running... remember when we came out of the circus that night. We got out quick because we didn't want to get stuck in the crowd and lose time?"

"Yeah."

"Remember there weren't a lot of people walking around the booths and rides and things?"

"Right. Everybody was inside watching the circus."

"There's a show today at two, so there probably won't be a lot of people walking around during the show."

"So?"

"So maybe the gypsy will take a walk and leave his tent if there aren't any people around to have their fortunes told. He can't stay in that tent all the time. I didn't even see a bathroom."

"Yeah, or a kitchen. He's gotta go eat someplace."

"Right. We watch, and when he leaves the tent, you go in and get the box."

"Yeah, I go... *I* go? What do you mean I go? Why don't you go? You should go. It's your idea."

Philip wondered whether he could trust Emery with an important job like this one. Emery might end up doing something dumb, like he usually did.

"All right. All right. I'll go. But you gotta be the lookout. If I'm in the tent, and you see the gypsy coming, you gotta let me know."

"I will."

"And no practicing. Only say he's coming if he's really coming. Got it?"

"I got it."

"The show's not until two o'clock. Let's go home for lunch. Come for me around one-thirty."

With that agreed upon, the boys crawled out of their secret lair and headed home.

CHAPTER TEN

The boys stood across the street from the entrance to Lighthouse Field and watched the crowds of people walking around the midway visiting the booths and rides before heading into the big tent to see the show. The boys spoke little, and when the people began to disappear into the big tent, they spoke not at all.

Finally, Philip said, "Let's wait until fifteen minutes after the circus starts and then go see."

Emery nodded, too tense to speak.

The time passed until Philip tapped his watch, and the boys crossed the street.

"Not many people walking around," Philip said. He looked toward the pharaoh's tent. "I don't see the pharaoh."

The pharaoh played some kind of card game with people who bet they could find the card with a picture of a pyramid on it after the pharaoh moved the cards around a table. If they found the pyramid, they would win a stuffed Egyptian snake. If they lost, they lost the money they paid to play. Philip thought the snake was cheap looking and wondered why anyone would want to win it. At the moment, the table the pharaoh set outside his tent to play the game on was missing, his tent flap closed.

"I don't think he's there," Emery answered. "Let's check on the gypsy."

They walked a few steps further and saw that the gypsy's tent looked empty too, with the flap closed and the table the gypsy used to tell fortunes nowhere in sight.

"Go see if he's home," Emery said.

"Suppose he is?"

"Then say we came to say hello."

The boys approached the gypsy tent. Philip cleared his throat and called, "Hello. Mr. Gypsy. Anybody in there?"

Nothing happened.

"Go peek," Emery said.

Philip, his heart pounding, pushed open the flap of the tent. He pushed it further.

"Nobody here," he reported.

"Go in. I'll watch," Emery encouraged.

Philip entered the tent and looked around. The gypsy's crystal ball sat on its usual table. Some gypsy clothing was tossed over a chair. A pair of gypsy shoes lay on the cot. The same handful of change and paperback book sat on the small table at the head of the cot. Philip moved his gaze below the cot. He didn't see the box. He moved in a slow circle, checking everywhere he could see. No box. Philip fell onto his knees and looked way under the cot. There it was! The box of jewelry sat pushed against the bottom of the tent wall. Philip heard the flap of the tent behind him and nearly screamed in horror. It was only Emery.

"I see them coming! The gypsy and the pharaoh. Hurry up!"

Philip knew he couldn't let the gypsy see him carrying the box out of his tent, so he pushed the box as hard as he could. The bottom of the tent was very tight against the ground, but using all the power he could call up, Philip managed to get the box under the tent and outside. A few pieces of straw came inside the tent when he pushed the box outside. Philip wriggled backwards from under the cot and paused to grab two quarters from the gypsy's spread of change on the side table. Then he rushed through the tent flaps to join Emery.

"They saw me," Emery reported. "Here they come."

Philip saw the gypsy and pharaoh coming their way. They'd seen him come out of the gypsy's tent.

"What are you two kids doing here?" the gypsy demanded.

"We... we..." Emery sputtered.

Philip saved him. "We came to see if you had anything else for us to do so we could get more wishes?"

"Yeah," Emery rapidly agreed. "Do you?"

"Three is all you get," said the pharaoh.

"Yeah, that's all," the gypsy chimed in. "Now get."

Philip and Emery obeyed gladly. They hurried out of the midway and across the street.

"Where's the box?" Emery asked. "You didn't get it?"

"I did. I pushed it out of the tent... look can you see... there. See the gigantic pile of straw?"

Emery looked and saw an elephant picking up batches of straw with its trunk and munching on it.

"Where the elephant is?"

"Yeah, I think the box is in the elephant straw."

"We can't get it there. We'll get stepped on by an elephant."

Philip shot Emery a don't-be-stupid look.

"*We* don't get it. We call the police again and tell them exactly where it is."

"We used up our money."

Philip pulled the gypsy's two quarters from his pocket.

"I took these from the gypsy's tent."

"Wow! You committed a robbery so we can report a robbery."

"Never mind that. Let's get to the phone."

The boys hurried back to the corner store.

"Stop here. Stop here," Philip ordered. "We gotta make sure nobody's watching the phone."

"Who would watch it?"

"The police, because of the stupid phone call you made."

Emery scrooched his face, but didn't argue. He joined Philip in scanning the area.

"See anybody?" Philip asked.

"Nobody," Emery answered in a sulking voice.

Philip ignored Emery's discontent and crossed the street.

"Keep watch again," he ordered as he dropped the two quarters into the slot. He knew it would be useless to try to disguise his voice the way Emery did. He would sound like a kid, no matter what he tried. So in his own voice he answered the operator's greeting.

"I can tell you where to find the box of jewelry that got stolen from Mrs. Healy on Van Kirk Street." He thought quickly and decided not to mention that an elephant stood guard over the box. It sounded way too crazy. "It's hidden at the circus right behind the tent of the gypsy in some straw. The gypsy and the pharaoh at the circus stole the box. Go arrest them. That's all I can tell you."

The operator started to ask a question, but Philip hung up the phone.

"Let's get away from here, Emery."

Philip walked quickly, Emery at his side. They turned at the first three corners they came to. Philip made the last turn in the direction of the circus.

"Where you taking us? I thought we were going to Mrs. Logan's bushes."

"Back to the circus the long way. We have to see what happens."

"You think they believed you?"

"They better. If they didn't, we're sunk."

"Even if the police show up, they may not find the box."

"Why not?" Philip asked perplexed.

"Maybe the elephant will eat it."

Philip stopped and stared at his friend.

"You really think an elephant is going to eat a big box of jewelry?"

"Well, he could pick it up and throw it somewhere when he finds out it isn't food. My sisters throw food on the floor if they don't like it. He may throw it someplace the police don't look."

"Your sisters aren't elephants. I don't know what the elephant's going to do. Let's just go watch."

A few moments later they had entered the midway at the opposite end from the tents of the gypsy and the pharaoh. They stepped lively until they reached a booth where you threw balls and tried to knock down puffy, cloth-covered wooden cats to win a prize. They could hear circus music playing in the big tent off to their left. They stepped behind the cat booth, but could still see the main entrance. They didn't have to wait long.

"Look, look, look," Philip cried.

Emery was still in a bad mood, a result of Philip's description of his phone call, but his attention rose quickly when he saw two police officers entering the midway.

"They're going to the gypsy's tent," Philip said softly.

"One's going behind the tent."

"He's talking to the gypsy. Look, the pharaoh is watching from his tent."

"Boy!" Emery exclaimed. "I wish we could hear what they're saying."

"He's coming back. Look! He's got the box! He's got it! He's putting it in a bag," Philip squealed. "Look at the gypsy!"

The police officer had showed the box, now safe in the clear plastic bag, to the gypsy. The gypsy's arms bounced up and down, and his mouth didn't stop as he tried to explain about the box to the police officer.

One of the officers turned and walked toward the pharaoh's tent. The pharaoh saw him and ducked back inside, but it didn't matter. The police officer went in and brought him out.

"They're taking them both away," said Philip, nearly jumping up and down.

"We did it!"

"*I* did it," Philip pointed out. "*You* made the dumbest phone call ever."

"It was *my* idea to make the phone call, wasn't it?"

"Yeah, but *I* made the phone call."

Emery could see he wasn't going to get the credit he thought he deserved. He gave up and said, "Let's go watch the police take them away."

The boys hurried down the midway and paused at the entrance. The gypsy and the pharaoh were already seated in the back seat of the police car behind the two policemen. The car started up and drove away.

Philip and Emery turned to one another, wide grins on their faces.

"We're safe," Emery declared.

"I hope so," Philip echoed.

CHAPTER ELEVEN

Philip and Emery spent the rest of Saturday as nervous wrecks. Twice the telephone rang in Philip's house, and he was sure the police were calling to ask for him. He watched his mother's face each time she answered the phone, hoping his stomach wouldn't explode from the tension he felt. But no calls came from the police. When he went to bed that night, Philip hoped tomorrow would go by fast so the circus could get out of town. There was one last show at two o'clock.

Around ten the next morning Philip looked up from reading the newspaper comics as his mother answered the phone again. His stomach took a roller coaster ride at his mother's words.

"How wonderful," Philip's mother said. She covered the mouthpiece of the phone and called to her husband, who lay on the sofa looking at other parts of the newspaper. "It's Mrs. Faraday. She says they found Mrs. Healy's missing jewels. At the circus, no less."

"I know," Philip's father answered. "I'm just reading about it."

Philip nearly gagged. The newspaper had the story! He bent his head over the comics so his eyes wouldn't meet his parents' gaze. They could usually tell when something bothered him. He kept listening to his mother's conversation, but all she kept saying was, "Really" and "Oh my" and "I see." He knew she'd report the conversation to his father as soon as she hung up, so he waited, staring at the comics page, but reading nothing.

"Mrs. Faraday seems to have the whole story," his mother said after she'd hung up the phone. "You'll never guess."

"I bet I can," Mr. Felton said. "It's all here in the paper. Gypsies and pharaohs and mysterious phone calls. Mrs. Healy must be happy."

"I'm sure she is, but she won't be back in her house for a while."

"Why not?"

"Mrs. Faraday says she has two sons, and she's going to live with one of them while the other tries to do something about her house. Clean it out so she can go back there and live. It must really be filled with junk."

"Junk to you; valuables to her."

"I guess, but still... Oh, well. Another neighborhood adventure comes to a successful end."

Philip's father raised the newspaper in front of his face, and the house grew quiet.

Philip knew he had to read the newspaper article, but his father didn't look like he'd be done with the paper anytime soon. Emery's two baby sisters always kept Emery's house disorganized. Maybe he and Emery could get the newspaper section they needed from his newspaper.

Philip rose and announced, "I'm going over Emery's awhile. Okay?"

"Sure," came his father's voice from behind the newspaper.

Philip headed out the door.

Fifteen minutes later Philip lay on his stomach in Mrs. Logan's bushes trying to get the speckles of light coming though the leaves to fall properly on his newspaper so he could read.

"Lemme see, too," Emery insisted.

"Oww! Watch your elbow. Stop pushing. Go over there. I'll read it to you, if you let me get the light on it."

Emery scuttled out of the way. "I saw the headline. *JEWEL ROBBERY THWARTED.* What's thwarted? Somebody had warts?"

"Your brain has warts. Quiet and listen.

"Police have thwarted a daring jewel robbery—thwarted has to mean they caught the bad guys—*thwarted a daring*

jewel robbery yesterday afternoon. Aided by two mysterious phone calls—that's us, Emery—uh, phone calls, the police arrested two circus performers, Frankie Fried who posed as a gypsy..."

"Posed!" Emery cried.

"That's what it says.

"But he made wishes come true. No way he was posing."

Philip frowned at Emery and continued "... posed as a gypsy and Karim Tugash, who posed as an Egyptian."

"Why'd you stop?" Emery asked.

Philip thought of the initials K-T he'd seen on the jewelry box. Not King Tut after all. He continued with the newspaper story.

"Both men operated booths in the circus sideshow on the midway. According to Police Captain Tim Auld, the two circus employees enlisted the help of two unwary young boys—that's us again, Emery—to steal a box of jewels, which they had pawned the year before when the circus came to town. They'd meant to reclaim the jewels themselves, but found out that someone else, Mrs. Healy from Van Kirk Street, had gotten them first.

"The two men, accomplished pickpockets, had managed to steal the jewelry from women who visited their sideshow acts. The police received their first clue when a mysterious phone call mentioned that a gypsy and a pharaoh had stolen the jewels, but no details were given by the caller, and the police considered the call a prank."

"You see, Emery. Your call was stupid. A prank. You didn't tell them anything."

"I said the gypsy and the pharaoh had the jewels, didn't I? How many gypsies and pharaohs we have in town, you think?"

Philip read on.

"A second phone call received later provided the necessary information for the police to locate the jewels and arrest the perpetrators. Perpetrators must mean the bad guys. The jewels have been returned to Mrs. Healy, and the circus will

have to do without its gypsy and pharaoh for a long time to come. The police believe the mysterious phone calls may have come from the two misguided children, who believed they would receive three wishes from the gypsy for helping them retrieve a magical, sacred scarab in the jewel box, a tale straight from The Monkey's Paw."

"Why do they keep talking about monkeys?" Emery wondered. "The computer said something about monkeys, too. The circus doesn't have any monkeys. And I'm *not* misguided."

"Maybe they mean you were as dumb as a monkey for believing you'd get three wishes, and being dumb as a monkey makes you misguided."

"Monkeys aren't dumb, and you believed it, too, didn't you? So you must be a misguided monkey, same as me."

Philip finished reading the article.

"The children may have finally caught on and were trying to correct their mistake. Captain Auld said the police were not seeking the children. On a final note, the box of jewelry did not contain a magical, sacred scarab."

"They're not looking for us?" Emery cried.

"That's what it says."

"Whew! Thank goodness. Hey, the magical scarab wasn't in the box. You think maybe it fell out in the lady's garage and is still there. Philip, if we had a magical scarab..."

"Right, we'd both be able to become witches."

Emery frowned. "I don't want to be a witch."

"Forget the scarab. I think the newspaper was making fun of us. There probably never was a scarab to begin with." Philip refolded the paper and said, "We better take this back to your house so your father doesn't wonder why we needed it."

The boys wriggled their way out of their bush hideout. They'd gone no more than a few steps before Emery stopped short and grabbed Philip by the arm.

"What?" Philip said, puzzling by the strange look on Emery's face.

"Our wishes."

Philip rolled his eyes.

"What wishes? There were no wishes."

Emery turned to his friend and shook his head slowly. "I don't know, Philip. I wished the old lady would get her jewels back and the gypsy and pharaoh would get arrested. Remember? Remember? And it came true. Both wishes came true. No, I think the gypsy is really a gypsy and has powers. You see both wishes came true, Philip. We still have a wish left. We can't waste it. We gotta try it."

"No, we don't."

"Yes, we *do* gotta try it."

"I mean we don't have a wish left. You wished for hamburgers and baked beans."

"What? *Argghh!* I wished for dinner at your house. I wasted our wish on chopped meat!"

"I don't think there really were any wishes, Emery."

"But three came true! I just showed you. What are you talking about? No, *four* came true! I wished for a circus ticket and got it."

"You said you didn't really wish. The gypsy *told* you you wished it."

"I *did* want to see the circus. I told you he read my mind. No, *five!* You wished for a circus ticket, and you got one!"

"You didn't hear me wish anything, did you? You were standing right next to me."

"You wished it before we went there. You know you did. When you found out I had a ticket. Right? Remember?"

Philip knew he did, so he only shrugged.

Emery began walking again, moaning over and over, "We wasted our wishes."

Philip wanted to argue about the wishes, but Emery's counting all the wishes that seemed to come true stopped him, and as they walked and Philip listened to Emery moaning about their lost wishes, he began to wonder whether he hadn't wasted the greatest opportunity of his life.

Philip and the Deadly Curse
DEDICATION

To Tyler Yeung

CHAPTER ONE

Where is it? Philip wondered in exasperation as he moved every book in his school desk from one side to the other. He'd lost *another* Jolly Rancher, the second this week. No one could have taken it because he hadn't been away from his desk all morning. Philip looked over his classmates to see whether anyone looked suspicious. His eyes finally settled on his best friend Emery, who sat directly across the aisle from him.

"Did you see my Jolly Rancher?" Philip whispered.

Emery shook his head and pointed to the front of the room.

"Did you lose something, Philip?" asked Mr. Ware, Philip's fourth grade teacher. "I haven't seen your head above the top of your desk for some time now."

"I thought I left something here, but I can't find it," Philip answered.

"May I ask what is so important it takes you away from what we're doing?"

"My Jolly Rancher."

Mr. Ware scrunched up his face. "You lost a happy farmer?"

The class giggled.

"No, no. It's candy."

"Candy. Well, if anyone sees Philip's candy, please return it to him. Now if you can return your attention to me, Philip, I'll be a jolly teacher."

Reluctantly, Philip sat up wondering if this bad luck of his would ever stop. Mr. Ware spoke to him nicely, but Philip knew when he'd been scolded; and he'd just been scolded. Where could his candy be? Philip began to slide down in his seat to look through his desk again, but caught himself. He'd already searched twice, and the next time Mr. Ware caught him, he would probably scold him with the louder voice the class never giggled at, and Philip had no desire to add more bad luck to his growing mountain of bad luck so he sat up and tried to pay attention. He couldn't, though. The only thing interesting his brain at the moment was the bad luck following him *everywhere* lately.

When Philip met Emery for their usual walk to school that morning, Emery said hello and immediately bent over to pick up a quarter from the grass right near Philip's left foot. Philip watched, astounded. Who knew how long the quarter had been lying there and how many times he had walked past it and not seen it? Emery shows up and one second later, he's a quarter richer. He considered telling Emery he had a hole in his pocket and the quarter slipped through and fell out, but Emery might ask to see the hole. Philip had no choice but to congratulate Emery on his lucky find and silently bemoan his own bad luck.

Now his candy had disappeared, and Philip was fed up with one piece of bad luck following another and another and another. What could he do about it? Nothing. He sat back dejectedly and listened to Mr. Ware drone on about common denominators.

Walking home with Emery later, Philip decided to share his problem with his friend.

"Emery," Philip began.

"Hold it," Emery cried and ran across the street. He bent down and picked up something, then ran back to Philip. A big smile on his face, Emery held up a hard, pink air ball. "Here, catch."

Philip grabbed the ball. "This is what you ran over there to get?" He bounced the ball and found it in very good shape.

"Didn't you see it laying right along the curb?"

Philip shook his head and handed the ball back to Emery, who shoved it into his coat pocket.

Philip looked at him in sad wonder and said, "You found a quarter this morning and a good ball this afternoon."

Emery shrugged and smiled. "Lucky, I guess."

"Yeah, but why? Today I lost my Jolly Rancher. Mr. Ware yelled at me. I lost another Jolly Rancher Monday. *I* didn't find the quarter, and *I* didn't find the ball. All *I* have is bad luck. Why?"

"Maybe you need a good luck charm, like mine," Emery said.

Philip stopped walking. "A good luck charm? You have one?"

Emery nodded. "Sure. Come on. It's cold."

"Show me," Philip said.

"I'll show you at my house. It's in my pocket. I don't want to undo my coat out here."

Philip wondered what could possibly be giving Emery all of this good luck.

CHAPTER TWO

"A troll?" Philip cried in surprise. "A *troll* is your good luck piece?"

Emery handed Philip a tiny plastic troll with long, frazzled yellow hair sticking straight up. "Yeah, but don't tell anybody. They'll tease me. It's an old toy my father saved from when he was a kid, and now it's my good luck troll." He took the troll back from Philip.

"Your father gave it to you?"

"Not exactly. I kept losing things here in the house. Want some candy?"

Philip took three pieces of chocolate wrapped in red foil from a red dish.

"Somebody gave this candy to my mother," Emery explained, "but I don't think she likes it much 'cause she never says anything to me when they disappear."

"She doesn't?" said Philip thoughtfully and took two more. "Tell me how you got your troll."

"I was looking for a piece to my chess game in the downstairs coat closet, and instead I found this troll."

"You never saw it before?"

"Nope."

"So how did it end up on the floor in the closet?"

"I guess it fell off the top shelf, and it couldn't have fallen off at a better time. I really needed some good luck."

"Yeah, well so do I." Philip mumbled eyeing the troll. "You never saw the troll before you found it on the floor?"

"Nope, never. I thought maybe somebody left it here, but I couldn't figure out who. My mother never lets me have anybody over to play because of the babies." Emery had two very small sisters. "Except you sometimes. You didn't lose the troll, did you?" A concerned look came over Emery's face.

Philip glanced longingly at the troll, but could not lie to his friend. "No, it isn't mine. I wish I had one, though."

Emery sighed in relief and shoved the troll into his back pocket. "Anyway, since I found it I've been having all kinds of good luck. Like today. You saw. I found my chess piece and lots of other things I lost. I only got yelled at once this week for making too much noise in the house around the babies; and I showed you the ninety I got on the math test. I never get even eighty usually."

"How do you know it belonged to your father?"

"He saw it and told me. I asked if I could have it, and he laughed and said I could."

Philip thought of his two missing Jolly Ranchers and his mouth watered. He looked at Emery's mom's bowl of chocolates and took two more pieces.

"*I* need a good luck piece. Can I look around your house?"

Emery shrugged. "Go ahead, but if you find anything that belongs to me, you have to give it back."

Philip frowned. "How do I know you won't just say it's yours if I find something good?"

"More bad luck for you," said Emery, laughing. "Pretty funny, eh? More bad luck."

"No, not pretty funny." Something about Emery's attitude made Philip angry. "I'm going to look in my own house. My house is as lucky as yours."

"Okay. Good luck."

Philip gave Emery a dark look. "Yeah, right." Philip slung his schoolbag onto his back and left, determined to find an even luckier good luck piece than Emery's dumb troll.

CHAPTER THREE

Philip decided to put things to a test right away and threw his schoolbag and coat on the floor by the front door. Now he had to find something to give him good luck, and find it before his mother noticed his coat and book bag. If the good luck charm prevented his mother from yelling at him to hang his things up, he'd know he'd found a genuine and glorious source of good luck. If his mother yelled anyway, it would prove what he found was only a worthless piece of luckless junk, and he'd have to keep looking. A happy thought came to him. Suppose he found something so lucky, his mother hung up his coat and schoolbag herself without even mentioning it! No good luck charm could be luckier than that!

Philip closed the front door softly so not to tip off his mother before he found his lucky charm. He tiptoed into the living room, got down on his knees in front of the sofa, and looked underneath it.

"Yuck," he muttered. He saw lots of dust and a few dark, mysterious, inviting shapes. Philip swatted at his nose. Every time he breathed out, dust bunnies leaped from the floor and spun in joy. He turned away, took a deep breath, and gritted his teeth. He pressed his eye to the space under the sofa and stretched his arm as far as he could. A new swirl of dust jumped inside his nose. "Ah-choo! Ah-choo!" He turned his head away and drew a deep breath.

"Philip, are you home?" came his mother's voice.

"Ah-choo! Ah-choo!"

"Aren't you feeling well? Are you getting a cold?" Philip squeezed his eyes shut and wiped the sneeze tears away.

"What are you doing? Get up off the floor." Philip's mother bent and felt his forehead. "No fever."

Philip yanked his arm out from under the sofa, and more dust leaped into the air.

"Philip, you're making all this dust... ah-choo! Ah-choo! Now you've got me sneezing, too. Get up from there."

Philip rose and brushed his arm off.

"Stop! You're making it worse," his mother said in a louder voice. "You left your coat and bag on the floor? You just threw them? You should know better. Go put them away."

"I... I was looking for something," Philip sputtered.

"Look for it someplace where there isn't so much dust. And *go* put your things away!" Philip's mother stomped from the room.

In his hand Philip held a strange green piece of plastic and a small black plastic horse with one leg missing. His mother reappeared with a broom and dustpan.

"Move away and let me sweep," she ordered.

Philip tossed the piece of plastic and the wounded horse on the floor where his mother could sweep them up. Obviously, neither one of them overflowed with good luck.

Philip hung up his coat and lugged his schoolbag to his bedroom. He tossed the bag on his bed and went to his secret shoebox. He took out a green Jolly Rancher to eat right away before he lost it.

As the candy melted in his mouth, Philip realized it wouldn't be an easy thing to find a lucky charm. Suddenly, an awful thought struck him. What if he needed some good luck to find a good luck charm? This confused Philip. If he had enough good luck to find a good luck charm, did it mean he already had good luck and didn't need a lucky charm? The more Philip considered, the more perplexed he became. He already knew he had bad luck—look at the day he had, losing candy and getting scolded by Mr. Ware. If that was the only kind of luck he had, he'd never find a good luck charm. But did he really need good luck to find a good luck charm? This puzzle made Philip's head hurt like it hurt when his father asked him: which came first; the chicken or the egg? Philip figured one of them had to, but which one since you couldn't have one without the other?

"Think about it," his father commanded and then walked away laughing.

If he could figure out which came first, he might figure out whether he needed good luck to find a good luck charm. Maybe Emery knew which came first. Philip went downstairs and phoned Emery.

"Hi, Philip. What do you want?"

"I want to know which came first. The chicken or the egg?"

"What?"

"I'm still trying to find a lucky charm, and I need to know which came first. The chicken or the egg?"

"Are you going to carry an egg in your pocket for good luck? What if it breaks?"

"No, I'm not going to carry an egg around. Don't be dumb."

"You're not gonna walk around with a chicken, are you?"

"What a stupid question! No, I'm *not* gonna walk around with a chicken. Where would I get a chicken?"

"The supermarket has them."

"Yeah, right. I'm gonna walk around with a dead chicken wrapped in plastic around my neck and expect to be lucky." Philip raised his voice, as often happened when he tried to have a serious discussion with Emery. "Listen, I need to know what came first. The chicken or the egg?"

After a moment of quiet Emery said, "Is it a boy chicken or a girl chicken?"

"What difference does it make?" Philip cried in exasperation. Why couldn't he ever get a straight answer from Emery?

"Because a boy chicken couldn't lay an egg so the egg had to come first 'cause it couldn't ever come second."

"So the boy chicken came from the egg?"

"No, it probably came from a farm."

"What do you mean, it came from a farm? Didn't the boy chicken come from an egg?"

"Only if there was a girl chicken who laid the egg, so the boy chicken wouldn't have been first or second. He would have been third."

"Who said anything about a girl chicken?"

"Me. There's gotta be a girl chicken. If there were only boy chickens there could never be any eggs. Boy chickens don't lay eggs."

"All right. All right. No boy chicken. It's a girl chicken. Which came first? The girl chicken or the egg?"

Emery thought a minute. "People eat eggs. Maybe the egg wouldn't last long enough to hatch a girl chicken because somebody scrambled it. So the egg had to come first."

"Who's talking about scrambling eggs? People eat chickens, too. Suppose the girl chicken got eaten; then there wouldn't be any eggs. So I guess the chicken came first."

"People don't eat live chickens."

"I know that!" Philip yelled into the phone.

"So if the girl chicken was alive to start with and nobody ate her, she'd lay eggs. So I guess the chicken came first."

"I just said that!"

Philip's mother called in to him. "Stop that yelling, Philip."

"So the answer's easy," Emery concluded. "If people ate the chicken there wouldn't be an egg. If people ate the egg there wouldn't be a chicken."

"Oh, that's the answer, you think? Everybody's eating everything and nothing came second?"

"I gotta go. You're making me hungry. See you tomorrow."

"Emery, just tell me what came first..."

Philip had a dial tone in his ear. He replaced the phone and decided that asking Emery for help proved he had the worst luck of anybody in the world. He decided he didn't care whether chickens or eggs came first or second as long as he found a good luck piece somewhere in his house. He'd keep looking.

CHAPTER FOUR

Philip sat on the edge of his bed to think. He knew all of the things in his room. If something in his room brought luck, he would already be having it. No, nothing in his room would be any help.

He thought back. Had anyone played over his house lately and left something behind? No, no one visited lately, and even if someone had visited, his mother probably already cleaned up and threw out anything she didn't recognize.

Philip walked down the hallway to his baby sister's room. Becky lay sleeping in her crib. She had a room full of toys, baby toys. Philip couldn't imagine good luck coming from anything a baby had slobbered on, so he proceeded on to the big bedroom at the end of the hall where his parents slept. The vacuum cleaner stood in the middle of the room, and cardboard boxes were spread out over the floor and the bed.

"Don't mess up in there," Philip heard his mother say from behind him as she climbed the stairs.

Philip stared into the room. "It's messed up already. What are you doing?"

Philip's mother peeked into the baby's room before joining Philip. "Shhh. Becky's still sleeping. I'll vacuum when she wakes up. I'm cleaning out the closets—the accumulated junk of the ages. How this all gets saved year after year is a mystery to me. Your father will have to go through this pile of junk and throw out whatever he doesn't want."

"If it's all junk, why would he want any of it?" Philip asked.

His mother gave him a look. "Junk to me is gold to him. If half of it gets thrown out, I'll declare it a victory."

"What is this stuff?"

Philip's mother sighed, shook her head, and rolled her eyes. "Memories of his childhood. Sentimental value, he says." She bent over a box on the bed and started separating the good from the bad. Philip knelt down on the floor next to his father's pile. He saw some old baseball cards of players he never heard of; a few old photographs of people he didn't know; and lots of meaningless other things. When he lifted a small notebook, something round and shiny and a little bigger than a quarter caught his eye. Philip picked it up with two fingers, and when he tilted it back and forth in the light, strange, creamy swirls seemed to move around on the surface. Dull silver metal covered the back.

"What's this?" Philip asked, holding the shiny disc up for his mother to see.

She glanced back. "From your father's stuff?"

"Yeah."

"You'll have to ask him when he gets home."

Philip stood up with the disc in his hand. When he turned toward the door, a flash of color from the top of his father's dresser caught his eye. Philip reached for it. A red Jolly Rancher!

"Where'd this come from?" Philip asked excitedly.

"I found it downstairs after you left for school. Here's another one." She reached into the pocket of her slacks and pulled out a yellow Jolly Rancher.

His two lost Jolly Ranchers! Philip took the candy from his mother and stared at the swirling, colorful disc in his hand. *Hmmmm.*

CHAPTER FIVE

"Philip," said Mr. Felton, "what you have in your hand is what I called my Moon Charm. My friends and I used it as a good luck piece when I was about your age. You know, like a rabbit's foot." The phone rang and Philip's father went to answer it, but Philip had heard all he needed to hear. This had to be the good luck charm he'd been looking for; and even better, a good luck charm that ran in his family!

The Moon Charm. Philip liked the sound of it so much he repeated it again and again—*The Mooooooon Charm*—as he waggled the shiny disc in the light. He headed for his bedroom, but stopped midway up the stairs as a wondrous and magical chill swept over him. With this charm he would never have bad luck again!

"I can't find my homework," Philip whispered to Emery next day when Mr. Ware asked the class to pass their homework forward.

"Did you do it?" Emery whispered back.

"Would I be looking for it if I didn't do it?" Philip reached into his pocket to touch the Moon Charm, but his pocket was empty! Panic shot through him! He didn't lose his Moon Charm already, did he? Life could not be so cruel to him; his bad luck could not be that powerful. But the Moon Charm was gone. What a disaster!

"I don't see your homework here, Philip." Mr. Ware said, thumbing through the papers from his aisle.

"I can't find it," Philip explained in a tiny voice. "But I did it." He shrugged.

"Give it to me tomorrow then, Philip." Mr. Ware smiled at him.

He's in an awfully good mood, Philip thought, puzzled. Could the Moon Charm have so much good luck that even from a distance it made Mr. Ware smile rather than scold? If it was that powerful Philip knew he had to find the Moon Charm and glue it to his arm if necessary.

Philip concentrated and tried to remember what he'd done with the Moon Charm that morning, but he couldn't picture doing anything with it. He reached down into his pocket and felt for a hole. No, no hole so the Moon Charm could not have dropped out. His homework and the Moon Charm had to be back in his bedroom. They better be, Philip thought, his stomach twirling in distress at the thought of losing the Moon Charm less than twenty-four hours after he found it.

Then Philip remembered! He'd taken the Moon Charm the night before and rubbed it over his homework, twice over the math he struggled with, to ensure he got everything right. He recalled putting the homework and the Moon Charm down on his desk when his mother called him to take a bath. Obviously, he forgot to put the homework back into his schoolbag and the Moon Charm back into his pocket. Philip watched the clock all day, counting the minutes until he could rush home and check.

Philip flew up the stairs when he reached home and there they were, lying on his desk—the Moon Charm and his homework! He stuck the charm deep into his pocket and put his homework into his schoolbag right away.

"Philip," Mrs. Felton called from downstairs.

Philip ran to the top of the stairway. "What do you want, Mom?"

"Emery's here. Come on down."

Philip felt his pocket again to check on the Moon Charm and then he went downstairs to his friend.

"Hi, Emery."

"Hi, Philip. What do you want to do?"

Philip thought a moment. He had never beaten Emery in chess. If he challenged Emery to a chess match and won, it would *prove* the Moon Charm's power... but maybe checkers might be easier. He beat Emery sometimes at checkers. Philip considered the possibilities and realized if he beat Emery at checkers, he wouldn't know whether the Moon Charm was the reason or not. Then he recalled he had never beaten Emery twice in a row at checkers. If he could win twice in a row, it could only be because of the Moon Charm's power. If it worked on checkers, then he could move up to chess.

"Let's play checkers," Philip suggested, slipping his hand into his pocket and giving the Moon Charm a twirl.

"Okay," said Emery.

As the boys climbed the stairs to Philip's room, Philip noticed Emery slip his left hand into his pocket. Ha! Emery had his troll with him and planned to use the troll's good luck power to help him win at checkers! It would be a battle between the power of Emery's troll and the power—the *super* power, Philip hoped, of his Moon Charm.

Philip set up the checkerboard, and Emery took the black pieces without comment. Yes! His first piece of luck, Philip realized, since he always preferred playing the red pieces. The charm was bubbling! Philip made the first move. Then Emery moved. Back and forth the game went. Soon, Emery had three kings left to Philip's two kings.

"What are you doing?" Philip asked when he saw Emery slip his left hand into his pocket again.

Emery pulled his hand out quickly. "Nothing. My leg itched. I think I got a rash."

Philip snorted in disbelief and moved his gaze to his two kings. His move.

"Hey, what are you doing?" Emery demanded.

Without thinking, Philip had slipped his hand into his pocket and let his fingers touch the Moon Charm.

"Nothing," Philip blurted and yanked his hand free.

"You put your hand in your pocket."

"My leg itches, too. You don't have the only itchy leg in the world, you know. I probably caught your stupid rash. Stop making noise and let me think." He moved one of his kings away from Emery's kings.

As Emery studied Philip's move, Philip noticed Emery's hand creep toward his pants pocket again.

"Hey, you already scratched your leg. It can't itch anymore."

"It's *my* leg. I can scratch it if I want to, even if it doesn't itch. Maybe I just want to keep it from itching later. Rashes are funny things."

"Well I can scratch *my* leg if I want to even if it doesn't itch and keep *my* leg from itching later, too. My rash is as funny as yours."

Each boy thrust a hand defiantly into a pocket.

With his free hand Emery made his move and trapped one of Philip's kings. Philip saw no matter what space he moved his king to, Emery would be able to jump him. He backed up his other king one space.

Emery took his hand out of his pocket, and when he did, Philip could see yellow troll hair poking out of Emery's fist.

"Hey!" Philip shouted and pointed an accusing finger.

Emery shoved his hand back into his pocket. "Hey what? It's nothing."

"Does your rash have yellow hair? It's your troll. Your good luck piece. You're using your good luck to try to win this game."

"So what?" Emery argued. "That's what a good luck piece is for, isn't it?"

Philip had had enough. Like a Wild West gunfighter he slowly drew his Moon Charm from his pocket and, with a sharp click, put it down on the table right in front of him. He looked Emery in the eye and said, "I don't care what you have. I have my own lucky charm now."

Emery stared at the glittery, shimmering disc. "What is it? Where'd you get it?"

"From my dad and it's a better good luck charm than a troll."

"I don't think so," said Emery. He reached into his pocket, pulled out his troll, and stood it next to the checkerboard. Emery studied the checkerboard and moved one of his kings toward Philip's untrapped king.

Philip backed his king away another space.

Emery moved his king closer.

After two more moves Philip's king ran out of back-up spaces, and both his men were trapped!

Emery smiled and returned his troll to his pocket. "You lose. I guess you better look for a different good luck charm. Yours doesn't work."

"It does work," said Philip with determination. "It just doesn't want to waste its power on something stupid like a checker game. You'll see. Wait till something really important comes along. You'll see how much good luck it gives me then."

Emery thought a moment. "How about tomorrow's spelling bee in school?"

Philip had forgotten and his spirits fell. Mr. Ware had promised to line the class up along the wall the next day and test them on how much spelling they'd learned. Philip knew he had not done a whole lot of studying. It would take a barrelful of good luck for him to do well in the spelling bee.

"Maybe we should both study a little," Philip suggested quietly. "You know. Help the good luck out."

"Okay, let's study till I have to go home for dinner."

"I'll go get the list of words," Philip said, the checker game forgotten.

CHAPTER SIX

Mr. Ware had given each student in the class a sheet of paper with four long rows of spelling words. Philip got his and said, "How shall we do this?"

"Let's do it like a real spelling test. Get paper and write one to ten. I'll say words and you write them. Then you do me."

Philip got some paper from his loose-leaf book. He numbered the test and said, "Go ahead."

Emery started at the top of column one. Philip listened and wrote as Emery pronounced each word. After the tenth word he pushed his paper across to Emery.

"Check it," he said.

Emery went back and forth between the test and the word list. When he finished, he wrote something across the top of Philip's paper and pushed it back to him.

Philip looked at what Emery had written. "Excellant."

"You got them all right," Emery congratulated. "Now do me."

Philip scanned the word list and gave Emery ten of the hardest words he could find. Emery wrote them down and pushed his paper back to Philip.

Philip examined the paper and a smile crept over his face. Emery watched as Philip put a big red *X* next to the word *serpent*. Emery had spelled it *serpant*.

"Oh," said Emery. "Sometimes I get *E*s and *A*s mixed up. Okay, you again."

Emery continued down the first column of words and time after time pushed Philip's paper back to him with *excellant* written across the top. Philip searched for the most difficult words on the list, and on each try Emery got one or two words wrong and Philip marked them with a big red *X*.

Finally, the boys got tired of testing, and Emery folded all his papers and put them into his pocket.

"What are you going to do with them?" Philip asked.

"Now I know which words I need to study. I just have to learn the words you put an *X* next to."

"Ha! I guess I don't have to study anything. I got everything right."

"Yeah, but you didn't do the hard ones you gave me or any of the words we skipped."

"Don't worry about me." Philip smiled and patted his pocket.

The boys parted.

The next morning Philip checked his pocket six times before he left for school. He checked his schoolbag for yesterday's homework and today's homework. Walking to school, he felt his pocket seven more times to be certain the Moon Charm hadn't fallen out.

Finally, in the middle of the morning, Mr. Ware said, "Clear your desks, everyone."

Philip put his math book away and checked his pocket again.

"Did you study after I went home?" Emery whispered.

"Nope, didn't need to," Philip boasted. He wondered how Emery would feel when the lame luck of his troll got him sent back to his seat where he could watch the Moon Charm power its way to victory.

Emery shrugged. "I studied some."

Mr. Ware's voice interrupted them. "Rows one, two and three line up along this wall. Rows four, five and six line up along the back."

Emery sat in row three and Philip sat in row four, so they separated. When they found their spots, their eyes met. Emery made a sly okay sign and tapped his pocket. Philip did the same back. The spelling bee began.

Some children dropped out on the very first round, but not Philip or Emery. They both made it through the second and third rounds. Philip anxiously wondered which would prove stronger: the Moon Charm or the troll.

Neither boy had a problem in rounds four and five, and when round five ended only six children remained standing. Philip saw Emery make a fist on the outside of pants pocket, and he knew Emery was squeezing his troll for good luck.

Mr. Ware smiled and said, "Let me congratulate the six of you for doing so well."

Philip made a fist outside of his pants pocket and wrapped his fingers around the Moon Charm. The solid feel of his shiny, magical disc gave him confidence. He knew his good luck would triumph over Emery's troll and allow him to spell any word the teacher came up with.

"We've used up the words from the list, but we'll keep going with words you haven't studied yet," Mr. Ware continued. "We'll test you on these surprise, difficult words until we get a winner. Philip, Julie, come on over and stand with the rest along the wall. Then we'll all be together."

Philip gladly joined Emery and the other finalists.

"Ready?" Mr. Ware asked. "Delicious."

Philip's heart dropped. Could he spell *delicious?* He knew the *shus* at the end would be tricky. Fortunately, he stood fifth in line, just before Emery, so maybe somebody would spell *delicious* by then.

The first two people, Mikey and Shelley, missed the word. Then Susan, the smartest girl in class, tried.

"d-e-l-i-c-i-o-u-s," she said.

"Good for you, Susan," said Mr. Ware.

Philip breathed easier. Thank heaven for Susan, the class brain.

"Tremendous," said Mr. Ware.

The next girl, Ellen, left out the *O* at the end of the word and had to sit down. Philip knew if *tremendous* wasn't spelled *U-S* at the end it had to be spelled with *O-U-S,* so he included the *O* and survived. Now only Susan, Philip, and Emery stood along the wall.

Philip squeezed the Moon Charm and wished for Emery to get a hard word. Mr. Ware said, "Accident."

Philip listened as Emery included both *C*s and put the *I* and *E* in the proper order. Mr. Ware congratulated him, and said, "Susan, back to you. Spell the word *excellent."*

Philip's eyebrows rose. He could see the word clearly before him! Good old Emery! He'd written the word six times for him yesterday on their practice tests! He held the Moon Charm tightly and hoped Susan botched the word.

Susan squished her eyes closed. "e-x-s-e-l-l... no." She paused. "e-s-x-e-... no."

"Time is almost up, Susan."

Philip squeezed the Moon Charm hard and thought, *Mess it up, Susan. Mess it up!*

He had to get that word—that oh-so-easy word!

Susan shook her head sadly, said, "I can't," and walked slowly back to her seat.

Thank you, Moon Charm! Thank you, Susan. Thank you, Emery!

"Very good try, Susan, but you may still have a chance. If both Emery and Philip misspell *excellent,* you'll come back up until we find a word only one of you can spell."

Susan nodded glumly.

Before Mr. Ware could even repeat the word to him, Philip blurted out, "e-x-c-e-l-l-a-n-t." He beamed a wide smile and waited for Mr. Ware's compliment.

"Oh, I'm sorry, Philip. That's close, but not quite right. You try, Emery."

Philip couldn't believe his ears. *That's not quite right?* He could see the word Emery wrote on his papers floating right before his eyes. What did Mr. Ware mean, *That's not quite right?*

Emery cleared his throat. "e-x-c-e-l-l-e-n-t." He and Philip both looked expectantly at Mr. Ware and waited.

"Yes!" bubbled Mr. Ware. "Very good, Emery. You are the class spelling bee champion. And your prize is..." Mr. Ware looked over the class to add to the suspense. "...you may take the weekend off from homework." A jealous groan came from the class.

Both boys returned to their seats and since there were only a few minutes until lunch, Mr. Ware let the children buzz about the contest and let off a little steam. Philip reached into his desk and pulled some papers out of his binder. He shook them at Emery and glared.

"What's the matter?" Emery asked.

"Look at these papers. You wrote *excellant* on these papers yesterday. Look, look. *Excellant. Excellant. Excellant.* Six times!"

"I know. You got everything right. They were excellent."

"Yeah, they were *excellent,* not *excellant.*"

"What do you mean they were *excellent,* not *excellant.* You're not making any sense."

"They're *excellent—E-N-T;* not e*xcellant—A-N-T.* Today I spelled *excellent* the way you spelled it yesterday—with an

190

A and not an *E*. Today you spelled it with an *E* instead of an *A*. You made me get it wrong. It's your fault. How come you couldn't spell it right yesterday, but today you can?"

Emery shrugged. "I told you. It's those *E*s and *A*s. Sometimes I get them mixed up, and sometimes they come out all right."

"I want to know: how come you mixed them up yesterday but they came out right today?"

Mr. Ware's voice interrupted. "Keep your voice down, Philip."

"You did this on purpose so you could win," Philip whispered fiercely.

"How could I do it on purpose?" Emery responded with a dismissive wave of his hand. "How could I know Mr. Ware would pick the word *excellent?* You heard what he said. The word's not even on our list. Maybe I just had better luck than you." Emery reached into his pocket and with a satisfied grin pulled the head of his troll out where Philip could see it.

Philip spun his head away, refusing to look at the awful troll. He hated admitting Emery was right. Emery couldn't have known what word Mr. Ware would pick, but his Moon Charm should have prevented him from picking the word *excellent.* The Moon Charm should have seen to it the teacher gave him a word he could spell. The Moon Charm should have made Emery spell *excellent* the right way *yesterday,* or the wrong way *today.*

Philip felt like taking out his Moon Charm and bouncing it off of Emery's head. What kind of stupid good luck piece would let a stupid old troll have more good luck than it did? This spelling bee with Emery's mixed up *E*s and *A*s was another gigantic dose of bad luck in his bad luck life.

Philip took a deep breath and thought a moment. Could there be something about the Moon Charm he didn't understand? Could there be something he had to say or do to make the Moon Charm work right? He didn't know, but his father should. His father would *have* to know, since he used the Moon Charm first. Philip decided he'd be waiting in the living room for his father when he got home from work that night.

CHAPTER SEVEN

Philip's father got home at his usual time and placed his briefcase in the usual spot inside the hall closet before going to say hello to his wife. When he fell into his favorite living room chair and opened his newspaper, Philip approached.

"Hi, Flipper," Philip's father greeted him. "Have a good day?"

Philip tossed the Moon Charm into his father's lap and said, "This thing doesn't work."

Philip's father folded his newspaper and put it aside. He picked up the Moon Charm and said, "What do you mean?"

"Emery has a good luck troll he found, and now he keeps having good luck. I wanted a good luck charm, too, and you gave me this Moon Charm, but it doesn't work. I still have bad luck. Emery found money on the ground; he found a new ball lying in the street; he won the checker game; and today he beat everybody in the whole class in the spelling bee, including Susan the brain. His troll works and this thing you gave me doesn't. It stinks."

Philip's father nodded and said, "Stinks, eh? Well, Flipper, I didn't tell you the entire story. I guess I better. When I was about your age, all the kids I played with had one of these. I seem to remember someone's father had a zillion of them, and he gave everybody one. I think the kid's father used them in his job and had a bunch left over. Anyway, we all got one, and everyone agreed it looked a lot like a tiny sun, the way it sparkles and shimmers."

"You called it a Moon Charm."

"I'm getting to that. So everyone called it their Sun Charm and went off and had some good luck with it, I guess. I don't remember anyone complaining. Except me. For some reason, I insisted on calling it a Moon Charm. I think I was having a big argument with my best friend Tommy Kelly over something. Anyway, if he said one thing,

I'd insist on the opposite, and he kept calling his disc a Sun Charm.

"I stubbornly insisted on calling it a Moon Charm, and that's when it started. My bad luck. I didn't get picked for teams until nearly last. I got into a fight with Tommy and got punished for ripping his shirt. I don't remember what all happened, but I remember nothing going right for a while. Didn't matter. I still refused to call the disc a Sun Charm like all the other kids."

Philip's father paused long enough for Philip to interject, "So you let me take it and use it? Thanks a lot, Dad. It's not a good luck charm. It's a deadly curse."

"You wanted it, so I let you have it. I kept on trying to get some good luck out of it, but before I could really test it, everybody got interested in other things, and somehow my charm ended up in the box where you found it."

"So you don't know whether it ever turned out to be good luck or not?" Philip asked in disappointment.

"I made a decision, Flipper. I realized I would have to make my own good luck and my own bad luck. I knew if I played well in games, I'd get picked for a team sooner. If I did my homework neatly, the teacher wouldn't yell me at. We can use all the good luck we can get, Flipper, but we can make a lot of good things happen ourselves if we just pay attention, work hard, and take care of the things we should take care of."

Pay attention? Take care of things? Work hard? Philip didn't like the sound of that.

"But good luck helps, doesn't it?" Philip asked, unwilling to give up on an easier pathway to success.

"Yes, I suppose it does."

"And you never really found out whether this Moon Charm ever changed to a good luck charm?"

"No, I can't say I ever did."

Philip weighed the two possibilities; hard work or being lucky. He had no trouble making a choice. He took the Moon Charm from his father and slid it back into his pocket.

"Maybe this thing starts slow and gets better," Philip suggested. "Maybe it needs to warm up."

"Looks like stubbornness runs deep on the male side of this family," Mr. Felton said with a smile.

Philip started across the room, but stopped and turned back to his father. "I'll let you know how it does."

"Philip, watch where you're going," said his mother, stepping around the corner from the kitchen carrying Becky in one arm and a bottle of milk in the other hand. "Pay attention. You almost knocked me over."

Philip looked at his father, who shrugged and said, "Might be a long wait."

Philip sighed and went up to his room.

CHAPTER EIGHT

"Everyone will be given a responsibility of some kind," Mr. Ware explained the next day in class. "And I know when we do our play for the rest of the school and for your parents, you'll all be wonderful."

Philip and Emery turned to look at one another. When, earlier that morning, Mr. Ware said he had a special announcement to make, each boy rubbed his pocket where his good luck charm rested and hoped it would be a class trip to someplace exciting. But a class play? Philip and Emery *hated* class plays. Making your costume; memorizing your lines; the teasing you got when you made a mistake; the embarrassment of standing on stage in the auditorium and having everyone look at you. Philip saw Emery take his troll out and hold onto it with both hands.

"I'm wishing I'll only have to make scenery or something easy," Emery whispered, and Philip noticed Emery's fists tighten around the troll.

Philip decided to wish for exactly the same thing—a nice easy job offstage. Philip quickly dug into his pocket and pulled out his Moon Charm. His stomach jumped when Mr. Ware took a paper off his desk and started to announce jobs. He squeezed his fist tight around his Moon Charm.

"The name of the play," Mr. Ware said, "is *The Seven Chinese Brothers.* You all know the story of how the Emperor tries to punish the brothers, but one brother takes another's place and each has a special talent that protects him from the punishment."

Philip moaned. He could just see himself in a long black wig with two ponytails hanging down his back. He might even have to put on makeup and wear one of those little red upside-down bowl hats. *Please not me,* he thought. *Not me! Not me! Not me!*

"Jason will play the Emperor." Philip had noticed how Mr. Ware had been very nice to Jason ever since wrongly accusing him of stealing some class money. "Annie will be the mother of the seven brothers. Beverly will be the princess the seven brothers like."

Philip grimaced. Beverly looked so weird he wondered how she'd get even one brother, Chinese or not, to like her, let alone seven.

"The seven brothers will be..." Philip rubbed his charm and closed his eyes.

"...Philip, whose power will be he can cry an ocean."

Philip's stomach dove to the floor, and he tuned out the rest of Mr. Ware's assignment of roles. Cry an ocean? He could cry an ocean all right, and do it right then and there. No self-respecting good luck charm would ever have let him be the first one—the very first—to be chosen to play a brother. He slipped the Moon Charm back into his pocket. Mr. Ware had stopped talking. Philip looked over at Emery, sitting and smiling happily. Emery turned to him and made an okay sign with his fingers.

Mr. Ware said, "Anyone who wasn't called will still have an important job making the scenery and decorations and will be on the top of the list to act in a future play we do."

From the corner of his eye Philip saw Emery turn and waggled his troll at him, but he refused to respond and stared stubbornly at the front of the room.

🐦 🐦 🐦

Philip was in a foul mood when his father got home from work.

"Hi, Flipper. How... ? Uh oh. Why such a long face? Not more bad luck, I hope?"

"Bad luck!" Philip burst out. "The worst bad luck ever. Mr. Ware announced a play today. *The Seven Chinese Brothers*. Then he announced what everybody had to do. I took out the Moon Charm and begged it for something to do off the stage. I didn't want a part in the play, and I most of all didn't want to be a Chinese brother."

"Don't tell me."

"I'm the Chinese brother who can cry an ocean—the *first* one he picked."

"How many lines do you have to memorize?" Philip's father had gone through this before when Philip had to act in a third grade play. He'd hoped then he'd never have to go through it again.

Philip shrugged.

"A whole lot?"

"Not so many."

"Well, Flipper, let's consider. You didn't want to get a big part, and you lucked out and got a small part. Sounds like good luck to me."

"I didn't want *any* part."

"Other kids have bigger parts than yours, right?"

Philip nodded. "The Emperor. The Princess."

"Okay. See, you're not the Emperor and you're not the Princess."

Philip shot a dark look at his father.

"More good luck," his father went on.

"Not being the Emperor's not enough good luck," Philip grumped. "Emery took out his troll and made the same wish as me. *He* got a job making scenery. That's what good luck is, getting what you want. His troll works. Your Moon Charm doesn't."

"Philip..."

The doorbell rang and Philip's mother went to open it. Emery entered the living room and Philip's mother continued upstairs.

Philip and his father looked at Emery.

In an uncomfortable voice Emery said, "Why are you both staring at me?"

Philip's father laughed. "Sorry, Emery. Philip told me about the school play. You're in charge of scenery, I hear."

"Not in charge. Just helping make it." Emery looked at Philip's unhappy face.

"I can't help it if the teacher picked me for scenery. He said there would be another play later. I'll probably have to be something on stage then."

"There, Philip," said Mr. Felton. "Emery is behaving very philosophically. His turn to be miserable will come later, and then it will be your turn to be happy."

"I want to be happy all the time," Philip grumbled.

Philip's father laughed. "Don't we all."

Emery went to the sofa and sat next to Philip. "I came over to help you learn your part."

"Very kind of you, Emery," Mr. Felton said. "Philip, you're *lucky* to have a good friend like Emery."

Philip scowled and said nothing.

"Cheer up, Flipper. With both Emery and me helping you learn your lines, you'll be a hit. You got through the play last year, and you'll get through this one. Do you have your script?"

"It's in my schoolbag."

"Go get it and let's take a look. And bring your Moon Charm, too."

Philip got his script and handed it to his father, who took the Moon Charm and leaned it against the lamp on the end table.

"It will watch over us from there, casting its good luck beams on all we do," said Mr. Felton. "Ready, Flipper?"

"I guess."

"Ready, Emery?"

Emery nodded.

"Let's get cracking. Your mother will have dinner ready soon."

CHAPTER NINE

Philip found he only had four lines in the play so by the time his mother called everyone for dinner, he had his part memorized.

"Well done. See, not so bad, eh? Since you know your part already," Philip's father said as they got up from the sofa, "I'll have time after dinner to give you some acting tips. It'll make you the star of the show. Want to stay for dinner, Emery?"

"What are you having?" Emery wanted to be sure he liked it. He ate dinner at Philip's house once when they had some kind of cabbagy thing he could hardly bring himself to look at, let alone eat. Luckily, he managed to pick out some pieces of ham sprinkled through the cabbage and didn't go home starving. If the cabbagy thing was on the menu tonight, Emery would head home fast.

"I'm not sure," Philip's father responded. "We'll find out soon."

Philip didn't care much about his father's promise to make him the star of the show. He could only think about how to make the Moon Charm into a dependable good luck piece. When he heard Emery ask about dinner, he thought of his own favorite food—spaghetti. He closed his eyes and rubbed his pocket. Suddenly, the aroma of spaghetti sauce tickled his nose!

"Come and get it," Mrs. Felton called. "Are you staying, Emery? I hope you like spaghetti."

Emery nodded and took a seat at the table across from Philip. "I do. As soon as I got invited, I hoped it was spaghetti." He leaned over and whispered to Philip. "With my troll."

Philip's spirits dropped. Emery's wish got them the spaghetti dinner, not his. But Philip refused to give up. His favorite dessert was mint chocolate chip ice cream.

He snuck his hand under the table and rubbed his Moon Charm in his pocket.

"What's for dessert, Mom?" he asked.

"We have a special dessert today," Mrs. Felton said with a smile as she put the spaghetti on the table.

Philip noticed Emery slip his hand beneath the dining table.

"I hope it's mint chocolate chip ice cream," Emery said. "I love mint chocolate chip ice cream!"

"Well, you *are* in luck. It's Philip's favorite, too, and I bought a gallon of it." Philip slapped the table in frustration. As long as he and Emery kept wishing for the same things, he would never know whose wish came true. As his mother spooned some sauce over his spaghetti, he tried to think of something Emery could not possibly wish for.

Ah! He had it! He closed his eyes, rubbed his Moon Charm, and wished his mother would go and visit one of her girlfriends after dinner. Whenever she went visiting, it left his father in charge, and he always got to stay up half-an-hour past his usual bedtime.

Emery went home after dinner, and Philip went up to his room to do his homework. When he finished, he came back downstairs. His father sat on the sofa giving Becky a bottle of milk.

"Where's Mom?" Philip asked. He crossed his fingers behind his back.

"She went over to Sally's house," his father answered, as he concentrated on feeding the baby.

Philip felt goose bumps pop out on his arms. The Moon Charm obeyed! That meant it *could* have been responsible for the spaghetti dinner and the mint chocolate chip ice cream. His Moon Charm was warming up!

Philip went to the kitchen and brought back the big bag of popcorn his mother'd bought at the supermarket. He sat down in front of the television to enjoy the evening.

Eventually, his father announced, "Time for bed, Flipper."

Philip looked at the clock. Whoa! A whole *hour* past his bedtime! More good luck. The Moon Charm was really cooking now! He went upstairs without an argument and cleaned himself up. Before slipping into his pajamas, he heard the phone ring.

"It's for you, Philip," came his father's voice from downstairs. "Emery."

Philip went into his parents' bedroom and picked up the extension.

"Hi, Emery. Why are you calling so late?"

"Hi, Philip. It's the homework. I didn't write down what math page we had to do, and my sisters have been crying all night. They fell asleep at last, and I can finally do my homework, but now I don't know what page to do."

Philip told Emery the page.

"Thanks, Philip. I was afraid you already went to bed so I wished on my troll you were still awake. See you tomorrow."

Emery hung up, but Philip stood like a statue, the phone against his ear. *Emery* wished for him to stay up late? Could Emery's troll be so powerful it knew *ahead* of time what wishes Emery would make? Could the *troll* have made his mother go out tonight? This could have been *Emery's* good luck again and not his.

Philip slowly lowered the phone to the cradle and went back into the bathroom to brush his teeth. After he got into his pajamas and climbed into bed, he stared at the Moon Charm leaning against a picture frame on his bureau. The moonlight coming through his window made the charm a swirl of colors.

It sure looks magical, Philip thought. All those wishes coming true tonight—Emery's troll, or his Moon Charm? He couldn't be sure, but he *had* to find out—he absolutely *had* to. How, though. How?

CHAPTER TEN

Philip's school scheduled Mr. Ware's play for a week from Thursday in the evening so parents who worked during the day could attend. Another class planned to sing some songs, and a third class would present a play about Thanksgiving. Philip's class began working on their play the next day. Mr. Ware assigned chores to the children who were not in the play, and he took the actors to the back of the room to see whether they knew their lines. Philip knew his, but some of the other children didn't seem to know anything. Philip rolled his eyes as Larry, the fourth Chinese brother, stood there opening and closing his mouth like a fish.

"Did you study your lines last night, Larry?" Mr. Ware asked in a gentle voice.

Larry opened and closed his mouth some more before he closed it and shook his head.

Philip rolled his eyes again. Larry always acted like this. He peeked toward the front of the room as Mr. Ware tried to impress on Larry the importance of not letting the other actors down. Emery lay on the floor coloring something and laughing with the boy lying next to him. He had the exact easy job Philip had wished for. Philip couldn't wait for the next play the class did so he could be the one coloring and laughing while Emery suffered through memorizing lines and saying them in front of an auditorium full of staring eyes.

"Well," Mr. Ware continued, "anyone who needs to read from the script, please take one, and we'll go through the play."

Philip shook his head when Mr. Ware offered him a script.

"Very good, Philip. I'm proud of you."

Mr. Ware's kind words made Philip feel a little bit better. He touched the Moon Charm in his pocket as rehearsal began, closed his eyes a second and wished he would remember his lines without any problem. When his turn came, he spoke his lines perfectly. Mr. Ware smiled at him and he felt a *lot* better.

At lunch Philip asked Emery, "Did you make any wishes with your troll today?"

Emery shook his head as he wiped the chocolate off his mouth from a piece of chocolate cake his mother packed for him.

"Not really."

"What's *not really* mean?"

"I only wished my mother wouldn't forget to put the chocolate cake in my lunch, but I knew she wouldn't anyway 'cause I reminded her a zillion times. I don't think I'd count that as a lucky troll wish, but maybe."

"You didn't wish I would remember my lines when we practiced the play, did you?"

Emery made a confused face. "Why would I waste a wish on something dumb like that? That should be *your* wish."

"Right," Philip muttered, relieved. Maybe the charm had *finally* started doing its job.

Two days later on Thursday, one week before the play, Mr. Ware brought the costumes into the classroom in a big box. Philip's stomach began to hurt when he saw what came out of the big box—little hats that looked like they belonged on a monkey, long braids of fake black hair, and shiny colorful coats for each of the seven brothers. Philip slid his hand into his pocket and wished with all his might he would not *feel* as silly as he knew he would *look* when he dressed up for the play.

"Philip, come up," said Mr. Ware.

Philip's stomach ping-ponged inside of him. Why did Mr. Ware always call his name first? He walked to the front of the room and stood with his back to the class.

"Turn around, Philip," said Mr. Ware.

Philip slid his hand into his pocket and turned around.

"First, the wig," Mr. Ware said with a grin.

Philip closed his eyes and felt the fuzzy, itchy black wig go onto his head. He felt the two braids dance down his back. He felt Mr. Ware put the elastic from the tiny hat under his chin.

"Now pick a coat, Philip. Whatever color you want."

Mr. Ware pointed into the big box, but Philip peeked at his classmates. It shocked him to see they were not rolling around on the floor laughing at him. He was even more shocked to find them looking at him with interest and even fascination on their faces.

Philip looked into the box and pointed to the gold coat. Mr. Ware took out the coat and helped Philip into it.

"Show everyone, Philip."

Philip turned to the class again. He heard some *oohs* and *aahs,* and even one *wow.* Two boys from the front row got out of their seats and came to rub their hands on Philip's soft, shiny sleeve. When Mr. Ware refrained from telling the two boys to sit back down, the rest of the class came to the front of the room and surrounded Philip.

Philip turned left and right, astonished by the attention. He stretched out his arms so more people could touch his coat.

"All right, everyone," said Mr. Ware. "Enough. Sit back down, and we'll dress the other Chinese brothers."

The class sat down muttering their approval of the costumes to one another, and the other six brothers chose their coats. The class watched, but no one came to the front to admire brothers two through seven. *Being first didn't turn out to be so bad after all,* Philip thought.

When everyone was in costume, the actors rehearsed the play in the classroom. Philip remembered his lines and surprised himself by feeling good about acting in the play. No, he felt *more* than good. He felt... fancy! He felt... important, standing in the front of the room in his golden costume saying his lines with everyone looking at him. He patted his pocket.

At lunch Emery slid next to Philip and said, "Those costumes look cool. I hope when I have to be in a play I get a costume as good as yours."

"Did you say *wow* when you saw me?" Philip asked. "Somebody said *wow.*"

Emery shrugged. "I don't remember. I don't think so."

Philip looked at Emery and said, "Did you wish for the costumes to be so good?"

"Why do you keep asking me if I'm making wishes about the play? I only made one wish—not to be in the play, and I got my wish."

Philip turned back to his peanut butter and jelly sandwich. He'd gotten *two* wishes he knew Emery hadn't wished for. His Moon Charm was coming through for him.

Every day until the next Thursday Philip's class rehearsed the play. Every day Philip felt a thrill when he put on his beautiful golden coat. Every day Philip recited his lines perfectly without even thinking about them.

"Are you nervous?" Emery asked as he and Philip walked home from school. "The show's tonight."

Philip shook his head. "No."

"You sure you're not nervous? Lots of people will be watching tonight."

"We practiced the play so much, tonight will be easy." Philip patted his pocket and made a quick wish to be sure. "Are you coming?"

"My mom wants to see it, so my dad has to stay home with the babies. I'd rather see the play than stay home with the babies, so I'll go with my mom."

When they reached Emery's house, the boys parted.

"See you tonight," Emery called. "And good..."

"Don't!" Philip cried. "Don't wish me good luck. Promise you won't make any wish about me or the play. Promise."

"Why?"

"Just don't," Philip insisted. "Promise."

Emery shrugged. "Okay, but then don't blame me if you mess up."

"I won't."

"You won't blame me, or you won't mess up?" Emery called after Philip, but Philip ignored him. As Philip walked, he considered the night ahead. He decided he'd make his wish right before the play began so the Moon Charm would have it fresh in its memory. He would hold his Moon Charm as tight as he could and wish for good luck for both the play and himself. Without Emery's troll in the way, this would prove once and for all whether the Moon Charm brought him good luck or not.

CHAPTER ELEVEN

All during dinner Philip practiced his lines inside his head. He thought of how he should walk on the stage, where he should stand, and how he should leave the stage. After dinner he watched TV—Mr. Ware had cancelled homework because of the play—while his mother fed Becky, who they planned to drop at Mrs. Moriarty's house so both his mother and father could see their son as the first Chinese brother.

"Everyone ready?" Philip's father asked.

"Almost," Philip's mother answered. "Let me get my coat. Here, Philip, take the baby a minute."

Philip sat on the sofa and his mother lowered Becky to him. Philip bounced her a little and a funny look came over the baby's face. All of a sudden Becky's mouth opened and some awful looking yellowy-green stuff came flying out as she threw up into Philip's lap.

"Ahhhhhh. Yuck! Help!" Philip cried.

"Oh my, Flipper," said Mr. Felton taking Becky into his arms. "Whoa. Bit of a mess."

"Bit of a mess! Dad, she barfed on me. She barfed all over me. What are you laughing at? It's so not funny."

"I'm sorry," Mr. Felton said, trying to hide his smile.

"What happened? Oh, Philip. I must have fed her too quickly. Don't move."

Philip's mother disappeared and came back with a roll of paper towels.

"Here, clean yourself off."

"Clean myself off! Suppose some of it gets on me. *Blaagh!*" Philip blurted at the thought of having Becky's used up, undigested dinner touch him.

"It's not radioactive, Philip," Philip's father said. "It just Becky's old food."

"Old food! Yeah, when dogs poop on the lawn, it's just old food..."

"Philip!" his mother cried. "Don't be so revolting."

Philip tore off a string of ten paper towels, rumpled them into a ball, and patted himself, carefully keeping his fingers well behind the paper towel.

"Get off what you can and go change your pants. Throw the dirty ones into the bathtub," his mother ordered.

"Hurry up, Flipper. The star of the show can't be late," said his father.

Philip did what he could with the paper towels and then rushed upstairs. He ripped off his wet, stained, smelly disgusting pants and tossed them into the bathtub. He ran into his room, grabbed another pair of jeans, put them on, and ran downstairs.

"Ready?" his father asked, smiling.

"I am. And stop laughing."

As everyone left the house, Philip checked his hands to make sure they were clean and dry and unspotted with Becky's... stuff.

🐁 🐁 🐁

Philip got into costume as he stood behind the stage curtain in the auditorium. He'd gotten to school barely on time. He watched everyone scurry around to get into position for the play. His class went on first so they had to be ready when the curtain rose. Philip walked to his spot and sat down. He could hear the audience chattering on the other side of the curtain. Behind him Mr. Ware told Kevin to speak loudly, and Philip reminded himself to do the same. Philip decided he'd waited long enough—it was time to make his wish. He patted his pocket and suddenly his body went cold, his head got hot, and he started to sweat. His pocket was empty! His Moon Charm was in the pocket of his throw-up pants, and his throw-up pants were lying in the bathtub at home, and the play was about to begin!

Philip tried quickly to recall his opening line, but it wouldn't come. All he could think about was his Moon Charm in the pocket of his pants covered with Becky's disgusting dinner.

"We start in two minutes," came Mr. Ware's voice.

Philip's heart pounded. His opening line. What was his first line? If he could remember the first line, maybe the other lines would come. Philip panicked when he saw the lights go out on the other side of the curtain. He heard the Chinese music Mr. Ware had on a CD and suddenly he felt like *he* had to throw up. The curtain rose and the eyes of the audience were on him.

Even though the auditorium lights were out Philip could still see the people in the light cast from the stage. So many people! Some people even stood in the back and along the sidewalls because the seats were filled. Philip's stomach began to ache. Oh, if he only had his Moon Charm. He looked inside his memory again for his first line but couldn't find it. His brain felt empty. Could he signal Emery to make a quick wish on his troll? He searched the audience.

Suddenly, the Chinese music stopped and the Emperor stood up and gave his first speech. The first brother's speech came next. Philip closed his eyes and looked for his opening line. The Emperor finished his speech. Philip rose, his mind a complete blank. He stared helplessly out into the audience. And then, like a miracle, the words came back to him.

"I am Chinese brother number one. I can cry an ocean of tears. This is my brother, Chinese brother number two."

Philip sat down and Ryan stood up. Philip felt his heart slow down. He saw the people in the audience smile. Philip listened carefully so he wouldn't miss his next turn to speak. The play went along exactly as they rehearsed it, except for mumble-mouth Kevin who nobody could hear.

Philip heard his cue and stood up again, walked in a circle, stood in front of the Emperor, and said, "Please let me go home to visit my mother before you kill me."

The Emperor made his reply, and Philip returned to his spot. Done! He'd said everything he had to. He stood in the right places at the right times. He was finished!

Relieved beyond measure and glad to be out of harm's way, Philip listened to the rest of the play. He stood when the rest of the cast stood and enjoyed the audience's applause. He and the rest of the actors bowed and gave a big wave good-bye just as Mr. Ware had showed them. Mr. Ware made a little speech about how hard the children had worked and the audience applauded again. The actors filed off the stage and took the front row seats left empty for them and settled back to watch the rest of the show.

When the performances ended, the children who acted in Philip's play went back to the classroom to get out of their costumes, and their parents met them there. Philip ran to his father. "Dad, I did it without the Moon Charm. I had it in my pants, but then Becky barfed on them, and I forgot to get the Moon Charm out of my pocket. And I almost forgot my lines, but right at the last minute I remembered them."

"Slow down, Flipper. You see, you remembered your lines because you worked hard to learn them. Remember what I said? Working hard makes its own good luck—a lesson I learned from the Moon Charm long ago. Now you've learned it, too. Another family tradition."

Mr. Ware interrupted. "Children, I have a surprise for you. Mr. Tolliver, Kevin's dad, has invited all the actors from the play out for some ice cream."

The children cheered and Philip smiled. Not even Emery's troll would get him this ice cream.

Mr. Ware announced the address of the ice cream parlor—the one in the mall—and everyone promised to meet there in twenty minutes.

CHAPTER TWELVE

Happy at how the evening turned out, Philip lay in bed in his pajamas studying the Moon Charm. He turned it over and over and watched the changing colors. His father knocked on the door and walked in.

"I wanted to come and say goodnight, Flipper," his father said. "Say goodnight and congratulate you on your spectacular stage performance."

Philip took the compliment in stride and looked thoughtfully at his father. He held up the Moon Charm and asked, "Dad, do you think it's good luck or not?"

"I think we both know the answer, Flipper. Not to beat a dead horse but—hard work makes its own luck. You studied your part in the play very hard, and that's why you were able to do it so well. You did do it without the Moon Charm, right?"

"Maybe you don't need the Moon Charm in your pocket all the time. Maybe it knows what you want and gives it to you no matter where it is."

"Philip, my boy, it was about at this point many years ago that I put the Moon Charm into the box where you found it, and there it rested all these long years." His eyes and Philip's eyes met, the important question dangling in the air. Philip's father shrugged. "Your guess is as good as mine."

Philip didn't want to guess. He wanted to *know*. "It's hard to tell what brings good luck and what doesn't."

"Truer words were never spoken, lad," Mr. Felton said with a smile.

"Close your eyes, Dad."

Philip's father obeyed the command, and Philip went to his closet and got out his secret shoebox, the shoebox both his parents promised never to open, even if they found it.

Philip took two Jolly Ranchers from his shoebox and put them under his pillow.

"Okay. Open your eyes."

Philip's father looked into the empty shoebox. "I thought you kept this thing filled with candy."

Philip gave a guilty smile and tried hard not to glance at his pillow. He dropped the Moon Charm into the shoebox where it landed with a small *plunk.*

"Well done. I congratulate you," his father complimented. "You've learned—we've *both* learned—you cannot depend on anything outside of yourself for good luck. You have to make your own." Philip's father extended his hand.

Philip looked at it.

"I want to shake your hand. You've taken a big step."

Philip shook his father's hand, and they both laughed.

"Get a good night's sleep, and I'll see you in the morning." His father left the room and went back downstairs.

Philip returned his candy to his shoebox and his shoebox to its hiding place. He hoped his father was wrong. How great would it be if he really had something to always bring him good luck? How easy things would be. He supposed he would have to do what his father said, though, and work hard to bring good luck to himself. Philip turned his lights out and crawled under the covers. With the comforting thought that the Moon Charm would be in his shoebox if he needed it for something special, Philip closed his eyes and thought back over his long and happy day.

About the Author

John Paulits is a former elementary school teacher. He has published numerous children's novels as well as numerous adult novels. You may visit his website for more details. www.johnpaulits.com. *The Empty Houses* (new) is John's nineteenth children's novel published by Gypsy Shadow. He lives in New York City and spends each summer at the Jersey shore.

WEBSITE: http://www.johnpaulits.com
BLOG: https://johnpaulits.wordpress.com/
FACEBOOK: https://www.facebook.com/john.paulits